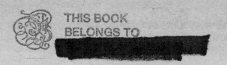
A Menu To Delight
THE MYSTERY GOURMET

For something light and piquant, we recommend *No Parking*, with its bewitching heroine and her three desperate suitors.

For a mouth-watering quick snack, you can try *Half a Clue*, in which Ellery Queen nabs the murderer almost before the victim has stopped breathing.

For a main course you can really sink your teeth into, there's Mum Is the Word, in which the "dying message" offers the ultimate in hidden clues.

And for an unforgettable *pièce de résistance*, we have *Abraham Lincoln's Clue*, a classic that Anthony Boucher called "perhaps the greatest of all Queen mysteries."

These are but four of sixteen great tales designed to please the most sophisticated palate—all prepared and elegantly served by the master chef of mystery, the one and only Ellery Queen.

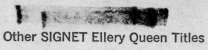

Other SIGNET Ellery Queen Titles

☐ **THE DUTCH SHOE MYSTERY** (#T3352—75¢)

☐ **THE EGYPTIAN CROSS MYSTERY**
(#T4084—75¢)

☐ **FACE TO FACE** (#P3424—60¢)

☐ **THE FINISHING STROKE** (#P3142—60¢)

☐ **THE FRENCH POWDER MYSTERY**
(#T4083—75¢)

☐ **THE GREEK COFFIN MYSTERY** (#T4085—75¢)

☐ **THE HOUSE OF BRASS** (#T3831—75¢)

☐ **QUEENS FULL** (#D2894—50¢)

☐ **THE ROMAN HAT MYSTERY** (#P3229—60¢)

☐ **THE SIAMESE TWIN MYSTERY** (#T4086—75¢)

☐ **ELLERY QUEEN'S ALL-STAR LINE-UP**
(#T3698—75¢)

☐ **ELLERY QUEEN'S CRIME CAROUSEL**
(#P3267—60¢)

☐ **ELLERY QUEEN'S MYSTERY PARADE**
(#Q3893—95¢)

Q. E. D.
Queen's Experiments in Detection

by **ELLERY QUEEN**

A SIGNET BOOK from
NEW AMERICAN LIBRARY
TIMES MIRROR

Library of Congress Catalog Card Number: 68-23847

The stories in this book originally appeared in the following magazines: *This Week, Argosy, Cavalier, Signature*—the Diner's Club Magazine, *MD,* and *Ellery Queen's Mystery Magazine.* Grateful acknowledgment is made to the editors.

This is a reprint of a hardcover edition published by the New American Library, Inc., in association with The World Publishing Company.

SIGNET TRADEMARK REG. U.S. PAT. OFF. AND FOREIGN COUNTRIES
REGISTERED TRADEMARK—MARCA REGISTRADA
HECHO EN CHICAGO, U.S.A.

SIGNET BOOKS are published by
The New American Library, Inc.,
1301 Avenue of the Americas, New York, New York 10019

FIRST PRINTING, JANUARY, 1970

PRINTED IN THE UNITED STATES OF AMERICA

Contents

THE PUZZLE CLUB

HISTORICAL DETECTIVE STORY

DYING MESSAGE
NOVELETTE

Mum Is the Word

December 31, 1964: The birthday of the new year and the old man became a fact at midnight. The double anniversary was celebrated in the high-ceilinged drawing room of Godfrey Mumford's house in Wrightsville with certain overtones not in the tradition. Indeed, in accepting the offerings of his family and his friend, old Godfrey would have been well advised to recall the warning against gift-bearing Greeks (although there had never been a Greek in Wrightsville, at least none of Godfrey's acquaintance; the nearest to one had been Andy Birobatyan, the florist, who was of Armenian descent; Andy had shared the celebrated Mumford green thumb until the usual act of God severed it).

The first Greek to come forward with her gift was Ellen Mumford Nash. Having gone through three American husbands, Godfrey's daughter had just returned from England, where she was in the fifth year of a record run with number four, an Egyptologist connected with the British Museum— the prodigal daughter home for a visit, her nostrils flaring as if she smelled something unpleasant.

Nevertheless, Ellen said sweetly to her father, "Much happiness, darling. I do hope you find these useful."

As it developed, the hope was extravagant. Her gift to him was a gold-plated cigaret case and lighter. Godfrey Mumford had given up smoking in 1952.

Christopher's turn came next. A little less than thirty years before, Christopher had followed Ellen into the world by a little less than thirty minutes. (Their father had never allowed himself to be embittered by the fact that their birth

7

had killed their mother, although he had had occasional reason to reflect on the poor exchange.)

Ellen, observing her twin over the champagne they were
all sharing, was amused by his performance. How well he did
the loving-son bit! With such talent it seemed remarkable that
dear Chris had never risen above summer stock and walk-ons
off Broadway. The reason, of course, was that he had never
worked very hard at anything.

"A real swinger of a birthday, father," Christopher was
saying with passionate fondness. "And a hundred more to
come."

"I'll settle for one at a time, son. Thanks very much."
Godfrey's hair was gray but still vigorous; his big body
tended toward gauntness now, but after seventy years he carried himself straight as a dancer. He was examining a silver-
handled walking stick. "It's really handsome."

Christopher sidled stage right, smiling sincerely; and Godfrey set the stick aside and turned to the middle-aged woman
standing by. She was small, on the dumpling side; the hands
holding the gift had the stub nails and rough skin of habitual
housework. Her face under the snowy hair lay quiet as a
New England garden.

"You shouldn't have gone to all this trouble, Mum," the
old man protested, "with the work you have to do around
here."

"Goodness, Godfrey, it was no trouble. I wish it could
have been more."

"I'm trying to remember the last time I had a hand-knit
sweater." Godfrey's voice was gruff as he fingered it. "It's just
what I need to wear to the greenhouse these days. When on
earth did you find the time?"

The sun came through to shine on the garden. "It's not
very elegant, Godfrey, but it will keep you warm."

It was over twenty-eight years since Margaret Caswell had
come to Wrightsville to nurse her sister Louise—Godfrey's
wife—in Louise's fatal pregnancy. In that time she had
brought into the world a child of her own, buried her husband, become "Mum" to the three children growing up in the
household—Godfrey's two and her one—and planned (she
had recently figured it out) more than thirty thousand meals.
Well, Godfrey Mumford had earned her devotion; he had
been a second father to her child.

She sometimes felt that Godfrey loved her Joanne more
than his own twins; she felt it now, in the drawing room.
For Godfrey was holding in his hands a leather desk set decorated with gold-leaf chrysanthemums, and his shrewd blue

eyes were glittering like January ice. The set was the gift of Joanne, who was watching him with a smile.

"You're uncanny, Jo," Godfrey said. "It's taking advantage of an old man. This is beautiful."

Jo's smile turned to laughter. "With most men it's supposed to be done with steak and potatoes. You're a push-over for chrysanthemums. It's very simple."

"I suppose people think *I'm* very simple. A senile delinquent," Godfrey said softly.

A frail little man with a heavy crop of eyebrows above very bright eyes hooted at this. He was Godfrey Mumford's oldest friend, Wolcott Thorp, who had formerly taught anthropology at Merrimac University in Connhaven. For the past few years Thorp had been serving as curator of the Merrimac University Museum, where he had been developing his special interest, the cultural anthropology of West Africa.

"I'll contribute to your delinquency, too," Wolcott Thorp chuckled. "Here's something, Godfrey, that will help you waste your declining years."

"Why, it's a first edition of an eighteenth-century compendium on mums!" Godfrey devoured the title page. "Wolcott, this is magnificent."

The old man clutched the tome. Only Jo Caswell sensed the weariness in his big body. To Wrightsville and the horticultural world he was the breeder of the celebrated Mumford's Majestic Mum, a double bloom on a single stem; he was a member of the Chrysanthemum Society of America and of chrysanthemum clubs in England, France, and Japan; his correspondence with fellow breeders and aficionados encompassed the globe. To Jo he was a gentle, kind, and troubled man, and he was dear to her heart.

"I'm grateful for all these kindnesses," Godfrey Mumford said. "It's a pity my response has to be to give you bad news. It's the wrong occasion, but I don't know when I'll have you all together under this roof again. Forgive me for what I'm about to tell you."

His daughter Ellen had an instinct for the quality and degree of trouble. By the flare of her nostrils she had sensed that what was coming was bad news indeed.

"Father—" she began.

But her father stopped her. "Let me tell this without interruption, Ellen. It's hard enough . . . When I retired in 1954, my estate was worth about five million dollars; the distribution in my will was based on that figure. Since that time, as you all know, I've pretty well neglected everything else in experimenting with the blending and hybridizing of mums."

Godfrey paused, took a deep breath. "I recently found out that I'm a fool. Or maybe it was fated. Anyway, the result is the same."

He glanced at the old book in his hands as if surprised to find it still there. Then he set it carefully on the coffee table and sat down on the crewel-fringed couch.

"I had put all my financial affairs in the hands of Truslow Addison's law firm. Where I made my mistake was in sticking with the status quo when Tru died and his son took over the practice. I should have known better. You remember, Christopher, what a wild youngster Tru Junior was—"

"Yes," said Christopher Mumford. "Father, you don't mean—"

"I'm afraid so," the old man said. "After young Tru died in that auto accident last May, the affairs of the law firm were found to be like a basket of broken eggs. You couldn't even make an omelet of them. Some of the funds in his trust he had simply gambled away; the rest vanished because of bad business judgment, stupid speculations, investments without rhyme or reason . . ."

His voice trailed away, and after a while the silence was cracked by the voice of Ellen Mumford Nash. Her slim and elegant figure was stiff with outrage.

"Are you saying, father, that you're without a *shilling?*"

Behind her Christopher made an abrupt move, extending his arm in a sort of forensic gesture, as if he were trying to argue away a legal point that threatened his whole case.

"You're joking, father. It can't be that bad. There's got to be something left out of so much loot."

"Hear me out," his father said heavily. "By liquidating assets I've managed to pay off all the creditors. This house and the property are mortgaged; there's not very much equity. I have an old annuity that will let Mum and Joanne and me live here decently, but on my death the income from it stops. I'll have to cut down my mums operation—"

Ellen broke in, bitter as the cold outside. "Damn your mums! If you'd stuck to growing seeds, the way you started, father, none of this would have happened. Left without a farthing? After all these years."

Godfrey had gone pale at her curse; otherwise his face showed nothing. He had apparently prepared himself well for the ordeal. "Your brother was right in one respect, Ellen. There is something valuable left—something that no one's known about. I want to show it to you."

Mumford rose and went over to the wall behind him. He pushed aside an oil painting of a vaseful of chrysanthemums, exposing a square-doored wall safe. His silent audience heard the faint clicking—more like a swishing—of a dial. He removed something, shut the door of the safe, and came back.

Ellen's breath came out in a whinny.

Her father's hand was holding up a magnificent pendant.

"You'll recall," the old man said, "that on my retirement I took a trip to the Far East to bone up on Oriental mums. Well, while I was in Japan I managed to get my hands on this beauty. I paid nowhere near what it's worth, although it cost me a lot of money. How could I pass this up? There are records authenticating it as a royal gift from the Emperor Komei, father of Meiji. It's known as the Imperial Pendant."

The gold links of the chain were exquisitely carved in the shape of tiny, intricate chrysanthemums; the pendant itself was a chrysanthemum, with an enormous diamond in the center surrounded by sixteen diamond petals. The superb gems, deep yellow in color, gathered the light in the room and cast it back in a shattering explosion.

"These stones are perfectly matched. The Emperor's agents searched the world to find enough of these rare yellow diamonds to complete the pendant. As a group, they're unique."

Ellen Nash's eyes, as hard as the gems, became slitted. She had never heard of Emperor Komei or the Imperial Pendant, but she was not invulnerable to beauty, especially when it had a high market value.

"Father, that must be worth a fortune."

"Believe it or not, it's been appraised at a million dollars." There was an arpeggio of gasps; and the warmth in Godfrey Mumford's voice expired, as if his pleasure had been chilled suddenly. "Well, you've seen it, so I'll put it back in the safe."

"For God's sake, father," cried Christopher, "not in a dinky little home safe! Why don't you put it in a bank vault?"

"Because I like to take it out every once in a while and look at it, son. I've had it here for a long time, and no one's stolen it yet. By the way, I'm the only one who knows the combination of the safe. I suppose I ought to leave a record of it, in case anything happens to me."

"I should think so!" said Ellen.

Godfrey's expression did not change. "I'll take care of it, Ellen."

He returned to the wall safe. When he faced them again, the painting hung in place and his hands were empty.

"So there's what's left of my estate," he said. "A piece of historic jewelry worth a million dollars." His fine face sad-

dened now, as if he had reached the limit of self-discipline.
"Wolcott, my old will included a bequest to you of a hundred
thousand dollars to finance that expedition to West Africa
you've always talked about."

"I know, Godfrey, I know," said Thorp.

"Now, when I die, I'm afraid your legacy will be only
one-fifth that."

Wolcott Thorp made a face. "I'm getting too old for expe-
ditions. Do we have to talk about these things?"

He said this in a mutter, as if the whole subject were painful to him. Godfrey Mumford turned mercifully to Margaret
Caswell.

"Mum, I originally planned a bequest to you and Joanne
of a quarter of a million dollar trust fund. Well, I'm not
going to make you suffer for my mistake after giving me half
your lifetime, at least any more than I can help. The inheritance tax will cut down the pie, but my new will takes ample
care of you in a revised trust. I wanted you and Jo to know
that."

He turned to Ellen and Christopher. "What's left, of
course, will go to you children, share and share alike. It isn't
what I'd planned, and I know it won't be what you expected,
but you'll have to make the best of it. I'm sorry."

"So," said Ellen with a little snap of her jaws, "am I."

"Oh, shut up, Ellen," her brother said.

And there was a silence.

It was broken by Joanne. "Well! Shall we drink a toast to
the birthday boy?" And she made for the rest of the champagne she had ordered from Dunc MacLean in the Square
(which was round), in High Village, leaving behind her a
definitely dismal New Year's Eve party.

January 1, 1965: Christopher Mumford was suffering
from an unfamiliar malady—some sort of malfunction of the
glands, as he diagnosed it. His mood had changed overnight.
He gulped a mouthful of air as cold and clean and heady as
Joanne's night-before champagne, and blew it out with a
happy snort, like a horse. Even the thought of his many creditors failed to depress him.

"What a scrumbumptious day!" he exulted. "What an absolutely virgin way to start the year! Let's mosey on up to the
woods beyond the greenhouse. I'll race you, Jo—what do you
say?"

Joanne giggled. "Don't be a chump. You'd fall flat on your
tunkus after twenty yards. You're in pitiful physical condition, Chris, and you know it. Dissipated, is what."

"You're right, of course. As dissipated as father's estate," said Christopher cheerfully.

"You could still repair the damage."

"Gyms make me dizzy. No, it's hopeless."

"Nothing is hopeless unless you make it so."

"Beware! Little coz is mounting her pulpit! I warn you, Jo, for some ridiculous reason I'm higher than the Mahoganies this morning. You simply can't spoil it."

"I don't want to. I *like* to see you happy. It's such a welcome change."

"Right again. In pursuance whereof, and since New Year's Day is the time for resolutions, I hereby resolve to restrict my coffin-nail intake, ration my poison-slupping, and consort only with incorruptible virgins, starting with you."

"How do you know I'm, well, incorruptible?"

"By me you are," said Christopher. "I ought to know. I've tried enough times."

"And that's a fact," said Jo in a rather grim tone. But then she laughed, and he laughed, too.

They skirted a big glasshouse, whose panes cast into the hard bright air a fireworks of sparks, and went on across a carpet of dead grass toward a noble stand of evergreens.

Christopher was happily conscious of Joanne beside him. Her stride was long and free, a no-nonsense sort of locomotion that managed to emphasize her secondary sex characteristics, which were notable. And not even the wool stockings and the thick-soled walking shoes could spoil as captivating a pair of legs as his connoisseur's eye had ever studied.

"You implied that I'm different when I'm happy," Christopher said.

"You certainly are."

"Well, I've been feeling different this morning, and I couldn't figure it. Now I can. I'm not different—I'm the same old swinger I've always been. What I am is, I'm responding to a fresh stimulus. You, cousin. It's you who spell the difference."

"Thank you, sir," said Jo.

"Oh, before this I've gone through the battlefield maneuvers with you, but I didn't actually *notice* you. You know what I mean?"

"I'm getting a clue," said Jo warily.

"But now I *am*. I mean I'm noticing *you*, cousin. In the aggregate, as it were, not merely here and there. Am I communicating? What does it mean?"

"It means you're bored, and you've decided to make a little time to while away your boredom."

"Not at all. Suddenly you've turned into a marvelously desirable piece of goods."

"And you're the susceptible buyer."

"Not the way you mean. You forget that I make my way boards-treading. I'm used to desirable women—the theater is lousy with them. So much so that I've been in danger of turning monk."

"Then why are you tickling my hand?"

"Because I've decided against celibacy. With your permission I'll go further. I'll put my arm around you."

"Permission denied. I've been through *that* maneuver before with you, and it leads to a major battle. We'll sit here on this log for a while and rest. Then we'll go back."

They sat. It was cold. They sat closer—for warmth, Joanne told herself.

"Gosh, it's wonderful," breathed Christopher in little puffs, like smoke.

"What's wonderful?"

"How things change. When we were kids I thought you were the world's biggest stinker."

"I couldn't stand you, either. There are times when I still can't. Like last night."

"Last night? Why, I was a model of deportment!"

"You don't know your father well, do you?"

"Father? As well as anybody."

"Your gift to him didn't show it. Nor Ellen's—Uncle Godfrey hasn't smoked in years. And you gave him a cane, for heaven's sake! Don't you realize Uncle Godfrey's too proud to use a cane? He'd never admit dependence that way."

Christopher Mumford had to admit to himself that her indictment was justified. He had bought the walking stick (on credit) without any real consideration of his father's needs or wants.

"You're right," he sighed. "What with handling father's correspondence and puttering around after him in the greenhouse, you've come to know him better than his own children."

They went on sitting on the log and holding hands. Jo had to hold his hands very firmly.

January 3: Breakfast was not a ritual at the Mumfords', but a certain deference was customarily shown to the head of the house. Family and guests, barring illness or improbably late hours the night before, were encouraged to present themselves promptly at 9:00, which was the time Godfrey Mumford invariably appeared.

Christopher, still floating in his euphoria, came downstairs a good twenty minutes ahead of schedule. He was astonished to find his distaff counterpart in the breakfast room before him. Ellen, the one member of the family traditionally AWOL from the morning meal, on this morning was lounging in a spot of sunshine with a cup of Margaret Caswell's rich coffee in her hand.

"I knew it, I knew it," Christopher said. "A day for miracles. Imagine finding you on your feet at this proletarian hour."

Ellen glared at him through the aromatic steam. "What makes you so cheerful of late? It's disgusting."

"Something rare has entered my life. As the ecclesiastical arm puts it, I have been uplifted in spirit."

Ellen sniffed. "You? Confessing to a tardy conversion? It would be too simply dreary."

"Hell, no, nothing so primitive." Chris spread himself over a chair and inhaled deeply of the delicious smells from the kitchen. "Although God knows neither of us has much to be cheerful about, I grant you."

"That's why I was hoping to catch you alone before breakfast." Ellen's tone expressed her resentment of the radical recourse forced upon her. "You may not realize it, Chris, but you've been pretty slimy lately. Is the sisterly eye mistaken, or aren't you being awfully attentive to our little country cousin? You aren't casting her for a role in some dirty drama you're working on, are you?"

"Don't be foul," said Christopher shortly. "And Jo's no yokel. Just because she hasn't had the advantage of living in London and acquiring a vocabulary of British clichés—"

"Bless my soul and whiskers." The saccharine in Ellen's smile was chemically combined with acid. "Lord Ironpants has suddenly developed a tender spot."

"Never *mind*. Just what did you want to talk about?"

"Father's performance the other night. What did you think of it?"

"Top hole, pip-pip, stiff upper, and all that."

"Do you suppose he was telling the whole truth?"

"Father? Of course. You know father isn't capable of a deliberate deception."

"I wonder," said Ellen thoughtfully.

"Don't be silly. He was giving it to us straight."

"Aren't you being terribly indifferent to it all? In my opinion, it's no trifle having your inheritance reduced from millions to thousands by your father's stupidity and the venality

of some crooked solicitor. There must be *something* we can
do about it."

"Sure—grin and bear it. It isn't as if we'll have to go on
relief, Ellen. There ought to be several hundred thou' at least
to be divided between us after taxes. In the parlance of
Wrightsville, that ain't hay."

"It 'ain't' five million, either. Honestly, I'm so furious with
father I could spit!"

Christopher grinned. Ellen's rage made her almost
human. "Chin up, old girl," he said, not unfondly. "It's the
Empiah tradition, y'know."

"Oh, go to hell! I don't know why I bother to discuss
anything with you."

Jo Caswell entered the breakfast room at the moment,
looking lusciously slim and young in a heather wool dress,
and bringing in with her, Christopher was prepared to swear,
a personal escort of sunshine. He immediately quit the natural variety for Jo's peculiar radiance; and Ellen, finding herself a crowd, withdrew disdainfully to the other end of the
table.

Jo's mother, starchily aproned, appeared in the doorway
from the kitchen. "Is Godfrey down?"

"Not yet, Mum," Jo said.

"That's funny. It's a quarter past nine by the kitchen clock.
He's always on time."

Ellen snapped, "Obviously, he's sometimes not."

Worry lines were showing between Mum's faded eyes. "In
all the years I've been here, your father's never been late for
his breakfast except when he was ill."

"Oh, for goodness' sake, Mum," said Jo, "he's probably
gone out to the greenhouse and lost track of the time. It isn't
as if it were two in the afternoon."

But Mum Caswell shook her head stubbornly. "I'm going
to look in his room."

"What a bloody bore." Ellen's impatience turned nasty.
"What about my breakfast? Am I expected to get it myself?"

"Perish the thought!" said Christopher, anticipating Jo.

Nevertheless, Mum hurried out. Ellen brandished her
empty coffee cup, ready to behead the peasant who had failed
to refill it. Christopher appeased his hunger by devouring
Joanne, who was trying valiantly not to let her dislike for
Ellen show.

Silence poured.

Until the cry from upstairs.

It was a cry raucous with urgency and terror. And then it
became a shriek, and the shriek repeated itself.

Joanne bolted for the doorway and vanished, Christopher at her heels. Ellen trailed behind, her face a curious study in dread and hope.

She came on the others midway up the staircase. Her aunt was clinging to the banister, her dumpling features the color of old dough. She managed a jerky thumb-up gesture, and Jo and Christopher sprang past her and disappeared in the upstairs hall. In a moment Jo was back alone, running down the stairs, past her mother, past Ellen.

"I've got to phone the doctor," Jo panted. "Ellen, please take care of mother."

"But what's the matter?" demanded Ellen. "Is it father? Has something happened to him?"

"Yes . . ." Jo flew for the phone. Ellen, ascending with an arm around Margaret Caswell's waist, heard the dial clacking, and then Joanne's urgent voice: "Dr. Farnham? Jo Caswell at the Mumford place. Uncle Godfrey's had a stroke, I think. Can you come right away?"

Dr. Conklin Farnham took the stairs two at a time. Mum, still dough-faced but recovered from the first shock, had insisted on returning to her brother-in-law's bedside; the doctor found her there. Christopher and Ellen, acting like trespassers, hung about in the hall outside their father's room, Joanne with them. They waited without words.

When Dr. Farnham emerged, his shoulders elevated in a chilling shrug. "He's had a stroke, all right. He's paralyzed."

"Poor pop," said Christopher. He had not called his father that in twenty years. "What's the prognosis, Doctor?"

"It depends on a number of things, most of them unpredictable."

"Any chance of a recovery from the paralysis, Dr. Farnham?" Joanne asked in a tight voice.

"The paralysis will gradually lift, but just how soon or how completely I can't say. It all depends on the extent of the damage. He ought to be in the hospital, but we're absolutely jammed just now, not a bed available, even in the wards. And I'd rather not risk the long jaunt up to Connhaven on these winter roads. So it looks like a home job, at least for now. He'll need nurses—"

"How about me?" asked Margaret Caswell, materializing in the doorway.

"Well." The doctor seemed doubtful. "I know you've done your share of patient-care, Mrs. Caswell, but in a case like this . . . Although it's true we haven't got an R.N. available right now, either . . ."

"I've taken care of Godfrey for over a quarter of a century," Mum Caswell said, with the obstinacy she showed in all matters pertaining to Godfrey Mumford. "I can take care of him now."

January 4–5: The first forty-eight hours after a cerebral thrombosis, Dr. Farnham told them, were the critical ones, which was all Mum had to hear. For the next two days and nights she neither took her clothes off nor slept; nor was there anything Joanne could do or say to move her from Godfrey Mumford's bedside, not even for ten minutes.

When the crisis was over, and the patient had survived—and was even making, according to the doctor, a sensational recovery—Jo and Ellen were finally able to pry Mum out of the sickroom and get her to lie down for a few hours. She fell asleep smiling triumphantly, as if she had scored a hand-to-hand victory over the Reaper.

Wolcott Thorp, apprised by Christopher of the stroke, drove down from Connhaven on the night of the fifth, looking like a miniature Russian in his old-fashioned greatcoat and astrakhan hat.

"Godfrey's all right, isn't he? He's going to live?"

They reassured him; and he sank into a chair in the foyer, beside the little table with the silver salver on it. "All my old friends are going," he mumbled. he was so pale that Joanne got him some brandy. "And those of us who survive feel guilty and overjoyed at the same time. What swine people are . . ."

It was some time before he was able to go upstairs and look in on the patient, who was being tended again by Margaret Caswell. For ten minutes Thorp chattered to his friend with desperate animation, as Godfrey stared helplessly back at him; until, clearing his throat repeatedly as if he himself had developed a paralysis, Thorp allowed Mum to shoo him out.

"It's too much to have to watch," Thorp told Jo and the twins downstairs. "I'm too big a coward to sit there while he struggles with that paralysis. The way he tried to talk! I'm going home."

"But you can't, Uncle Wolcott," said Jo, giving him the courtesy title she had used since childhood. "It's started to snow, and the report on the radio is that it's going to be a heavy one. I'm not going to let you take that long drive back over slippery roads. The plows won't even have had time to go over them."

"But Joanne," said the old curator weakly, "I have a huge day tomorrow at the Museum. And really, I'd rather—"

"I don't *care* what you'd rather. You're not leaving this house tonight, and that's that."

"Jo's right, you know," Christopher put in. "Anyway, Uncle Wolcott, you don't stand a chance. This is the new Joanne. Look at that chin, will you?"

You look at it," said his sister Ellen. "Oh, hell, why did I ever come home? Who's for a snack?"

January 6: The snow had fallen through half the night. From the kitchen window Christopher could look out across the white earth, an old bed with fresh sheets, past the glasshouse to the woods, where the conifers stood green among the sleeping nudes.

From behind him came a rattle of pans and the homely hiss of bacon; all around him, creeping like woodsmoke, lay warmth. Making the sounds and evoking the smells was Joanne; when her mother had turned nurse, Jo had taken over the housekeeping and cooking chores. Chris had promptly given himself the KP assignment for breakfast.

It was not a morning for fantasy; the day was too clear, the smells too real—it should have happened on a black night, with wind tearing at the house to an accompaniment of creaks. But, as Jo and Chris later agreed over clutched hands, perhaps that was what made it so creepy—the dreadful nightmare striking on a crisp morning to the smell of frying bacon.

For at the very instant that Christopher turned away from the window with a wisecrack about to part his lips—at the very instant that he opened his mouth—he screamed. Or so it seemed. But it was a fantastic coincidence of timing. The scream was hysterically feminine and originated upstairs. It was repeated and repeated in a wild fusillade.

Jo stood fixed at the kitchen range with the long fork in her hand; then she cried, *"Mother!"* and flung the fork down and ran for the doorway as if the kitchen had burst into flames. And Chris ran after her.

In the hallway stood Wolcott Thorp, one leg raised like an elderly stork, caught in the act of putting on his galoshes in preparation for his return to Connhaven. The curator was gaping at the staircase. At the top of the flight sagged Margaret Caswell, hanging on to the banister with one hand, while her other hand clawed at her throat.

And as she saw Jo and Christopher, Mum screeched, "He's dead, he's dead," and began to topple, ever so slowly, as in a film, so that Joanne, streaking past old Thorp, was able to catch her just before she could tumble. And Christopher followed, bounding up the stairs. He collided with his sister on the landing.

"What is it?" yelled Ellen; she was in a hastily donned robe. "What in God's name has happened now?"

"It must be father." Christopher dodged around her, shouting over his shoulder, "Come on, Ellen! I may need help."

In the hall below, activated at last, Wolcott Thorp hopped for the phone, one unhooked galosh flapping. He found Dr. Farnham's number jotted on a pad for ready reference and dialed it. The doctor, located at Wrightsville General Hospital, where he was making his morning rounds, would come at once. Thorp hung up, stared for a moment at the telephone, then dialed Operator.

"Operator," he said, swallowing. "Get me the police."

Chief of Police Anselm Newby cradled the phone cautiously, as if it might respond to rougher treatment by snapping at him, like a dog. He inclined his almost delicate frame over his desk and fixed bleak eyes, of an inorganic blue, on his visitor. The visitor, relaxing on the back of his neck, had the sudden feeling that he was unwelcome, which was ridiculous.

"Ellery," said Chief Newby, "why the hell don't you stay in New York?"

Ellery slid erect, blinking. "I beg your pardon?"

"Where you belong," said the Chief in a rancorous tone. "Go home, will you?"

A manifest injustice. Home, thought Ellery, is where the heart is, and for many years he had had a special coronary weakness for Wrightsville. He had arrived in town only yesterday on one of his spur-of-the-moment visits; and, of course, the very first thing this morning he had sought out the Chief in police headquarters at the County Court House Building.

"What," Ellery inquired, "brings this on? Here we were, wallowing in remembrance of things past, warm as a pair of tea cozies. In a moment I become *persona non grata*. It's obviously the telephone call. What's happened?"

"Damn it, Ellery, every time you come to Wrightsville a major crime is committed."

Ellery sighed. It was not the first time he had been so indicted. Before Newby's tenure there had been the salty old Yankee, Chief Dakin, with his sorrowful accusations. It's a continuing curse, he thought, that's what it is.

"Who is it this time?"

"They've just found Godfrey Mumford. That was a friend of his, Wolcott Thorp, on the phone, to notify me of Mumford's murder."

"Old Mumford? The Chrysanthemum King?"

"That's the one. I suppose there's nothing I can do but invite you along. Are you available?"

Mr. Q, rising slowly, was available, if with reluctance. His Wrightsville triumphs invariably left an aftertaste of ashes.

"Let's go," said Wrightsville's perennial hoodoo.

Christopher, dressed for the snow, blundered on Joanne on his way to the front door. She was crouched on the second step of the staircase, hugging her knees. Jo had not cried, but her eyes were pink with pain.

"You need fresh air," prescribed Christopher. "How about it?"

"No, Chris. I don't feel like it."

"I'm just trundling around the house."

"What for?"

"Come see."

He held out his hand. After a moment she took it and pulled herself up. "I'll get my things on."

Hand in hand they trudged around the house, leaving a double perimeter of footprints in the deep snow. Eventually they came back to where they had started.

"Did you notice?" Christopher asked darkly.

"Notice? What?"

"The snow."

"I could hardly not notice it," said Joanne. "I got some in the top of one of my boots."

"Tracks."

"What?"

"There aren't any."

"There are, too," said Jo. "A double set. We just made them."

"Exactly."

"Oh, stop talking like a character in a book," Jo said crossly. "What are you driving at?"

"*We* left a double set of footprints," said Christopher. "Just now. But nobody else left any. Where are the tracks of the murderer?"

"Oh," said Jo; and it was a chilled, even a tremulous "Oh" —like a little icicle preparing to fall to bits.

They stood there looking at each other, Jo shivering like a scared and forlorn child.

He opened his arms. She crept into them.

It was Ellen who answered the door. She had used the short wait to recover her poise; she had, so to speak, raised the Union Jack. Chief Anselm Newby stepped in, followed by Ellery.

"You're the Chief Constable," Ellen said. "The last time I was in Wrightsville, Dakin was Constable."

Newby received this intelligence with a displeasure that even Ellen Nash recognized. In Anse Newby's glossary, constables were exceedingly small potatoes, found in tiny, dying New England villages.

"Chief of Police," he corrected her. Professionally he used a quiet voice, with an occasional whiplash overtone. He evidently felt that this was such an occasion, for his correction flicked out at her, leaving a visible mark. "The name is Newby. This is Ellery Queen, and he's not a constable, either. Who are you?"

"Mrs. Nash—Ellen Mumford Nash, Mr. Mumford's daughter," said Ellen hastily. "I've been visiting over the holidays from England." This last she uttered in a defiant, even arrogant, tone, as if invoking the never-setting sun. It made Newby examine her with his mineral eyes.

The tension Ellery detected under the woman's gloss was clearly shared by the group huddled in the entrance hall behind her. His glance sorted them out with the automatic ease of much practice. The handsome young fellow was obviously the brother of the constable-oriented Anglophile, and he was (just as obviously) feeling proprietary about the grave and lovely girl whose elbow he gripped. Ellery became aware of a familiar pang. What quality in Wrightsville is this, he thought, that it must cast in every murder melodrama at least one ingénue with a special talent for touching the heart?

His glance passed on to the snow-haired lady, fallen in with exhaustion; and to the little elderly gentleman with the jungle eyebrows and the musty aura of old things, undoubtedly the Wolcott Thorp who had accounced the finding of the body to Anse Newby over the phone. Newby, it appeared, knew Thorp; they shook hands, Thorp absently, as if his thoughts were elsewhere—upstairs, in fact, as indeed they were.

When the Chief introduced Ellery, it turned out that some of them had heard of him. He would have preferred anonymity. But this was almost always the toe he stubbed in stumbling over a skeleton in some Wrightsville closet.

"Rodge and Joan Fowler were talking about you only a

few weeks ago," Joanne murmured. "To listen to them, Mr. Queen, you're a cross between a bulldog and a bloodhound when it comes to—things like this. You remember, Chris, how they raved."

"I certainly do," Christopher said gloomily. He said nothing more, and Ellery looked at him. But all Ellery said was, "Oh, you know the Fowlers?"

"*That* Queen," said Ellen. Ellery could have sworn, from the way her nostrils flared, that he was giving off unsocial odors. And *she* said nothing more.

"Well," the Chief of Police said in a rubbing-the-hands tone of voice, "where's the body? And did anybody notify a doctor?"

"I did, just before I telephoned you," Wolcott Thorp said, "He's waiting in Godfrey's bedroom."

"Before we go up," suggested Ellery—and they all started —"would you people mind telling us how the body was found, and so on? To fill us in."

They told their stories in detail, up to the point of the call to headquarters.

Newby nodded. "That's clear enough. Let's go."

So they went upstairs, Margaret Caswell leading the way, followed by Newby and Ellery, with the others straggling behind.

The old man was lying on the floor beside his bed. He lay on his back, his eyes fixed in the disconcerting stare of death. The front of his pajama coat was clotted with the seepage from the knife wound in his chest. There had been very little bleeding. A black-handled knife trimmed in what looked like nickel protruded from the region of his heart.

"Hello, Conk," Ellery said to the doctor, but looking at the corpse.

"Ellery," Dr. Farnham exclaimed. "When did you get to town?"

"Last night. Just in time, as usual." Ellery was still looking at the dead man. "How's Molly?"

"Blooming—"

"Never mind Old Home Week," said Newby irritably. "What's your educated guess, Doctor, as to the time he got it?"

"Between four and five A.M., I'd say. A good spell after the snow stopped, if that's what you're thinking of."

"Speaking of the snow," said Ellery, looking up. "Who made that double set of tracks around the house I noticed on driving up?"

"Joanne and I," said Christopher from between his teeth.

"Oh? When did you make them, Mr. Mumford?"

"This morning."

"You and Miss Caswell walked all around the house?"

"Yes."

"Did you notice any tracks in the snow other than those you and Miss Caswell were making?" After a moment Ellery said, "Mr. Mumford?"

"No."

"Not anywhere around the house?"

"No!"

"Thank you," Ellery said. "I could remark that that's very helpful, but I can understand that you ladies and gentlemen may have a different point of view. It means no one entered or left the house after the snow stopped falling. It means the murder was committed by someone *in the house*—someone, moreover, who's still here."

"That's what it means, all right," said Chief Newby with undisguised satisfaction. He was inching carefully about the room, his bleak glance putting a touch of frost on everything.

"That was intelligent of you, Chris," Ellen Nash said viciously. "So now we're all under suspicion. What a bloody farce!"

"You've got the wrong category, I'm afraid," her brother said morosely. "As one of us, I suppose, is going to find out."

There was a dreary moment. Jo's fresh face held a look of complete incredulity, as if the full meaning of the trackless snow had just now struck home. Ellen was staring over at his recumbent father, her expression saying that it was all his fault. Margaret Caswell leaned against the door, her lips moving without a sound. Christopher took out a pack of cigarets, held it awkwardly for a moment, then put it back in his pocket. Wolcott Throp mumbled something about the absolute impossibility of it all; his tone said he wished he were back in his museum among the relics of the legitimately dead.

"The knife," Ellery said. He was looking down again at Godfrey Mumford's torso. "The fact that the killer left it behind, Newby, undoubtedly means that it's useless as a clue. If it had any fingerprints on it, they probably were wiped off."

"We'll dust the room and knife for prints, anyway," said the Chief. "Don't any of you come any further than that doorway . . . Not that it's going to do us any good, as you say, Ellery. You people—I take it you've all been in this bedroom in the last day or so at one time or another?" He shrugged at their nods.

"By the way," Ellery said, "I haven't seen one of these old-fashioned jackknives in years. Does anyone recognize it? Mrs. Caswell?"

"It's Godfrey's," Mum said stiffly. "He kept it on the writing desk there. It was one of his prized possessions. He'd had it from childhood."

"He never carried it around with him?"

"I've never seen it anywhere but on his desk. He was very sentimental about it . . . He used it as a letter opener."

"I have a boyhood artifact or two myself that I'm inclined to treasure. Did everyone know this, Mrs. Caswell?"

"Everyone in the household—" She stopped with a squeak of her breath—like, Ellery thought, a screech of brakes. But he pretended not to notice. Instead, he knelt to pick something up from the floor beside the body.

"What's that?" demanded Chief Newby.

"It's a memo pad," Dr. Farnham said unexpectedly. "It was kept on the night table at my suggestion for notations of temperature, time of medications, and so on. It apparently fell off the table when Mr. Mumford toppled from the bed; he must have jostled the table. When I got here the pad was lying on the body. I threw it aside in making my examination."

"Then it doesn't mean anything," the Chief began; but Ellery, back on his feet, staring at the top sheet of the pad, said, "I disagree. Unless . . . Conk, did Mr. Mumford regain any mobility since his stroke?"

"Quite a bit," replied Dr. Farnham. "He was making a far better and faster recovery than I expected."

"Then this pad explains why he fell out of bed in the first place, Newby—why, with that knife wound, he didn't simply die where he lay after being struck."

"How do you figure that? You know how they'll thrash around sometimes when they're dying. What does the pad have to do with it?"

"The pad," said Ellery, "has this to do with it: after his murderer left him, thinking he was dead, Godfrey Mumford somehow found the strength to raise himself to a sitting position, reach over to the night table, pick up the pencil and pad —you'll find the pencil under the bed, along with the top sheet of the pad containing the medical notations, where they must have fallen when he dropped them—and blockprinted a message. The dying message, Newby, on this pad."

"What dying message?" Newby pounced. "Let me see that! Had he recovered enough from the paralysis, Doc, to be able to *write*?"

"With considerable effort, Chief, yes."

The dead man's message consisted of one word, and Newby pronounced it again, like a contestant in a spelling bee.

"MUM," he read. "Capital M, capital U, capital M—MUM."

In the silence, fantasy crept. It made no sense of the normal sort at all.

MUM.

"What on earth could Godfrey have meant?" Wolcott Thorp exclaimed. "What a queer thing to write when he was dying!"

"Queer, Mr. Thorp," Ellery said, "is the exact word."

"I don't think so," said the Chief with a grin. "It won't do, Ellery. I don't say I always believe what's in front of my nose, but if there's a simple explanation, why duck it? Everybody in town knows that Mrs. Caswell here is called Mum, and has been for over twenty-five years. If Godfrey meant to name his killer, then it's a cinch this thing on the pad refers to her. No embroidery, Ellery—it's open and shut."

"What—what *rot!*" Joanne cried, jumping to her mother's side. "Mother *loved* Uncle Godfrey. You know what you are, Chief Newby? You're a—you're a nitwit! Isn't he, Mr. Queen?"

"I would like to think about it," said Mr. Queen, staring at the pad.

January 9: It is a fact that must be recorded, at whatever peril to his reputation, that Mr. Queen had achieved in Wrightsville the status of a professional houseguest. In more than two decades he had proved a miserably meager source of revenue to the Hollis Hotel. No sooner did he check in, it seemed, than he was checking out again. Let it be said in his defense that this was not the result of parsimony. It was simply because of his flair for entangling himself in Wrightsville's private lives and, as a consequence, being invited to Wrightsville's relevant private homes.

The invitation to move over to the Mumfords' was extended by an unhilarious Christopher at the iron plea of Joanne. Jo's motive was transparent enough; Ellery was not sufficiently vain to suppose it had anything to do with moonlight and roses. With Chief Newby breathing down her mother's neck, Jo had sensed an ally; she wanted Ellery not only on her side morally, but physically at hand.

Which explains why, on the morning of January ninth, Ellery settled his account at the checkout desk of the Hollis and, lugging his suitcases like ballast on either side, tacked briskly toward the northwest arc of the Square. Crossing Upper Dade Street, he luffed past the Wrightsville National Bank, Town Hall, and the Our Boys Memorial at the entrance to Memorial Park, and finally made the side entrance of the County Court House Building. In police headquarters he paused long enough to register his change of address with Chief Newby, who received the announcement with an unenthusiastic nod.

"Any luck with the fingerprinting, by the way?" Ellery asked.

"All kinds of it. We found *everybody's* fingerprints in the bedroom. But not a one on the jackknife. Wiped clean, all right." Newby scowled. "Who'd have thought a nice little housekeeper like Mum Caswell would have the know-how to remove her prints or wear gloves?"

"If you're so certain she killed Mumford, why don't you make the collar?"

"On what evidence? That MUM message?" The Chief threw up his hands. "Imagine the corned-beef hash a defense lawyer would make of *that* in court. Ellery, find something for me in that house, will you?"

"I'll do my best," said Ellery. "Although it may not turn out to be for you."

"What do you mean?"

"I'm concerned with the truth, Anse. You're merely concerned with the facts," said Ellery.

And he left before Newby could reply.

Ellery commandeered a taxicab driven, to his surprise, by someone he did not recognize, and was trundled off (after circling the Square) back up broad-bottomed State Street to the oldest part of town, where the houses were black-shuttered pre-Revolutionaries set well back on rolling lawns in the shade of centuries-old trees. And soon he was ringing the chimes-doorbell of the Mumford mansion.

It was the day after Mumford's funeral, and the big house was still haunted. The old man's presence seemed to linger in the sight and scent of his precious chrysanthemums, which in lesser greenhouses bore their blooms from late August to December.

Joanne let him in with a glad little cry.

She established him in a tall-ceilinged bedroom upstairs with a tester bed and a beautiful Duncan Phyfe highboy that he instantaneously coveted. But he was made melancholy by the vase of two-headed mums that Jo had set on the night table, and he soon descended in search of fleshlier company.

He found Jo, Ellen, and Christopher in the library, and it became clear at once that the exercise of his peculiar gifts, at least as far as Ellen Nash was concerned, was her charge for his lodging.

"I'm not going to dignify for one moment the absurd conclusion that one of us murdered father," Ellen said. "He was done in by some maniac, or tramp, or something—"

"The snow," her brother said damply.

"To hell with the snow! What I'm interested in is that father left a million dollars' worth of pendant in his wall safe, and I want that safe opened."

"Pendant?" said Ellery. "What pendant?"

So Christopher told him all about the New Year's Eve party, and what Godfrey Mumford had told them, and how he had exhibited the Imperial Pendant to them and then returned it to the safe.

"And he also told us," Christopher concluded, "that he was the only one who knew the safe combination. He said he was going to make a note of the combination for us. But we haven't looked for it yet."

"I have," said Ellen, "and I can't find it. So that your stay here won't be a complete waste of time, Mr. Queen, why not show us how Superman detects? A little thing like finding a safe combination should barely test your reputation."

"Do we have to worry about the pendant *now?*" asked Jo.

"It shouldn't take too long, Miss Caswell," said Ellery. To himself he was saying: Maybe a million dollars' worth of jewelry has something to do with where Godfrey's boyhood knife had finally rested.

Searches were Ellery's forte, but this one defeated him. Trailed by relatives of the deceased, he squanderd the rest of the morning looking in obvious places. But unlike Poe's purloined letter, the combination of the safe was nowhere to be found.

They took time out for lunch and an inventory of the unlikelier places, and the afternoon passed in exhausting this inventory. Then time out again, and over dinner a round-table discussion of other possibilities, however remote. Mr. Queen's fame as a sleuth underwent reappraisal by at least one conferee present. And Mr. Queen himself grew audibly more quiet.

After dinner Ellen returned to the search of the files she had already ransacked once. Ellery, reminding himself bravely in the face of his failure that there was, after all, more than one way to flay a kitty, took Christopher aside.

"I'm prompted," Ellery announced, "to go directly to the source of the problem—namely, to the safe itself. Can you show me where the blamed thing is?"

"What do you have in mind?" asked Christopher. "Nitro?"

"Nothing so common. A bit of fiddling with the dial, à la Jimmy Valentine."

"Who's he?"

Ellery said sadly, "Never mind."

Christopher led him to the drawing room and, turning on the lights, went to the chrysanthemum painting on the wall and pushed it aside. Ellery began to flex his fingers like a violin virtuoso before a recital.

He studied the thing. The safe door was about ten inches square and in the middle was a rotating dial about six inches in diameter. Etched into the circumference of the dial were twenty-six evenly spaced notches numbered in sequence 1 to 26. Around the dial Ellery saw a narrow immovable ring or collar in the top of which was set a single unnumbered notch —the notch used for aligning the numbers of the combination when opening the safe.

In the center of the dial was a bulky knob, about half the diameter of the dial itself, and on the knob was etched the manufacturer's trademark—an outline of the god of metal-working, Vulcan; around the rim of the knob appeared the manufacturer's name and address: VULCAN SAFE & LOCK COMPANY, INC., NEW HAVEN, CONN.

The safe door was locked. Ellery duly fiddled with the dial, ear cocked à la Jimmy Valentine. Nothing happened—at least, to the safe door. What did happen was the entrance into the drawing room of Ellen, in a sort of half excitement, trailed by a disdainful Joanne.

"Ah, the ladies," said Ellery, trying to cover up his chagrin. "And have you found the combination to this stubborn little brute?"

"No," Ellen said, "but we've found this. Maybe it'll tell you something."

Ellery took the sheet of paper. It was a bill of sale for the wall safe.

"Dated nine years ago." He pinched his nose, which was itching. "Must have been ordered just after he got back from that trip to the Orient you told me about, when he acquired the Imperial Pendant. Especially ordered, then, to be the repository of the pendant. Invoice tallies—same name and address of manufacturer; terse description, 'Wall safe per order.'"

"That's it," said Christopher. "No doubt about it."

"Is it important, Mr. Queen?" asked Jo, in spite of herself.

"It could be mighty important, Miss Caswell. While I have fiddled and burned, you may have discovered a treasure."

"Then you have better eyes than I," said Ellen. "Anyway, where do we go from here?"

"Patience, Mrs. Nash. Chris, I want you to take a trip to New Haven. Check out the safe company and learn everything you can about this particular model—details of the original order, any special instructions accompanying the order —and, yes, check the price, which seems very high to me. Also, the Vulcan Company may have the combination on file, which would simplify matters. If they don't, hire one of their experts to come back with you, in case we have to force the safe.

"Meanwhile, you two girls keep searching for a record of the combination. Cover every room in the house. Not excluding the greenhouse."

January 11: Christopher's return taxi from the Wightsville airport produced a clamor. Jo flew into the foyer from the direction of the kitchen, followed by Mum; Ellen descended from upstairs in jumps. Ellery, a lonely stag, was meandering among the red spruce and birch outside; and Joanne, booted and mackinawed, was dispatched to fetch him.

Assembled in the drawing room, they saw from Christopher's expression that he was no courier of good news.

"Briefly," Christopher told them, "the Vulcan Safe and Lock Company, Inc., no longer exists. The plant and all its files were destroyed by a fire in 1958. The firm never went back into business. Fellow sufferers, I return to your bosoms with nothing—not a clue, not a record of anything connected with the purchase of the safe."

"The high price," Ellery asked, frowning. "Did you remember to check the price?"

"Right. I did. And you were. Right, I mean. The price father paid was just about twice what safes of similar size and type were bringing the year he ordered it. It's funny that father would let himself be skinned that way. He may have been careless about his lawyer, but he was a good enough businessman, after all, to have made millions in packaged seeds before he went chrysanthemum-happy."

"There was nothing wrong with your father's business sense, Chris," said Ellery. "Nothing at all." And his eyes promptly went into hiding.

Ellen, who held a more cynical view of her late sire, was

clearly of the opinion that the father's simplicity had been passed on to his son. "Didn't you at least bring back a safe expert to open the bloody thing?"

"No, but I got in touch with another New Haven safe outfit, and they'll send a man up as soon as I phone them."

"Then do it. Put through a trunk call right now. What kind of fool are you?"

Christopher's ears had turned a lovely magenta. "And you, sister mine, you're a greedy little devil. You're so hot to lay your hands on that pendant that you've lost the few decent instincts you used to have. You've waited this long, can't you wait another couple of days? Father's hardly settled in his grave."

"Please," murmured Mum.

"Please!" cried Jo.

His reflections disturbed by the sibling colloquy, Ellery roused himself. "It may not be necessary to call in anybody. Your father left a dying message—MUM. Chief Newby is positive that Godfrey was leaving a clue to his killer's identity —Mum Caswell here. But if Godfrey meant to identify his murderer, why did he choose to write MUM? MUM can mean a great many different things, which I shan't go into now; but, as an identification, it's an ambiguity. Had he wanted to accuse Mrs. Caswell, he could simply have written down her initials, MC. If he'd meant to accuse Joanne or Mr. Thorp—JC or WT. One of his children? 'Son' or 'daughter' —or *their* initials. Any one of which would have been specific and unmistakable.

"I choose to proceed, then," Ellery went on, "on the assumption that Godfrey, in writing MUM, did not mean his killer.

"Now. What had he promised to leave for you? The combination of the safe containing the only considerable asset in his estate. So his dying message may have been meant to be the safe combination. If so, the theory can be tested."

Going to the painting, he pushed it aside. Entranced, they trooped after him.

"Study this dial for a moment," Ellery said. "What do you see? Twenty-six numbered notches. And what does twenty-six suggest? *The number of letters in the alphabet!*

"So let's translate M-U-M into numbers. M is the thirteenth letter of the alphabet, U the twenty-first. Safe combination: 13-21-13. Now first we twirl the dial a few revolutions —to clear the action, so to speak. Then we turn to 13 and set it directly under the alignment notch—there. Next we turn the dial to the right—we'll try that direction first—and align

the 21. And now to the left—usually the directions alternate
—back to 13."

Ellery paused. The crucial instant was at hand. There was
no movement behind him, not even a breath.

He took hold of the knob and pulled, gently.

The thick, heavy door of the safe swung open.

A shout of triumph went up—and died as if guillotined.

The safe was empty. Utterly. No pendant, no jewel box,
not even a scrap of paper.

Later that day, true to his commitment, Ellery visited Anse Newby at police headquarters and reported the
opening of the safe, including its emptiness.

"So what have you accomplished?" the Chief growled.
"Somebody killed the old man, opened the safe, swiped the
pendant. That doesn't knock my theory over. It just gives us
the motive."

"You think so?" Ellery squeezed his lower lip. "I don't.
According to everyone's testimony, Godfrey told them he was
the only one who knew the combination. Did one of them
figure out the M-U-M combination before I did and beat me
to the safe? Possible, but I consider it unlikely, if you'll pardon the self-puff. It takes experienced follow-through thinking to make the jump from M-U-M to 13-21-13."

"All right, try this," argued Newby. "Somebody sneaked
downstairs in the middle of that night and got lucky."

"I don't believe in that sort of luck. Anyway, it would call
on one of them to be a mighty good actor."

"One of them is an actor."

"But, I gather, not a good one."

"Or maybe she—"

"Let's keep it a neutral 'he.' "

"—maybe he forced old Godfrey to tell him the combination before sinking the knife into him."

"Even less likely. Everyone knew that Godfrey's paralysis
included his speaking apparatus, which even in a good recovery is usually the last to come back, if it comes back at all.
Certainly no one could bank on the old man's being able to
talk suddenly. Did the killer order Godfrey to write the combination down, under threat of the knife? Even so, Godfrey
would have been a fool to do it; his daughter not withstand-
ing, he seems to have been very far from a fool. He'd have
known he was a goner the moment he wrote it.

"I'll admit," scowled Ellery, "that all these unlikelihoods
don't make for exclusive conclusions. But they do accumulate
a certain mass, and the weight of them convinces me that the

killer put Mumford out of his misery simply to hurry up the
inheritance of the pendant, not to steal it; that the killer then
left, and Mumford wrote M-U-M on his own."

"You talk all-fired pretty," said Chief Newby with a grin.
"There's only one thing."

"And that is?"

"If the killer didn't swipe the pendant, where is it?"

"That," Ellery nodded morosely, "is Bingo."

"I don't mean to high-hat my betters," twanged Newby,
"but you have to admit you've got a tendency to bypass the
obvious. All right, you hit on M-U-M as Godfrey's 13-21-13
safe combination. But why does that have to have anything to
do with his reason for writing MUM on the pad? He was a
bug on mums, so it was natural for him to use M-U-M as the
combination. But he could have meant something entirely different when he wrote M-U-M on the pad. I still say he was
fingering his murderer. And when you have a suspect around
who's actually known as M-U-M, and called Mum, what more
do you want?"

"Mum Caswell isn't the only obvious referent."

"Come again?"

Ellery's reasoning organ, needled by a phrase Newby had
used, was busy with its embroidery.

"A bug on mums, you say. My point is, it's absolutely bi-
zarre and incredible that MUM should have been his dying
message. MUM is the symbol of the man who wrote it. He
was a famous horticulturist specializing in mums. Everything
about the man said MUM, from the flowers in his greenhouse to the oil paintings and prints and sculptures and intag-
lios and jewelry and Lord knows what else of them throughout the place. MUM was Mumford's trademark: a mum is
on his stationery, as I've taken the trouble to check; also on
his wallet, and on his car, and in wrought iron over the front
entrance. The moldings and doorknobs are all decorated with
carved mums. And did you notice that his shirts sport an em-
broidered mum instead of his monogram? Also, if you'll pardon me, there's the irony of the knife that took his life, Godfrey's boyhood knife. How many times, allow me to wonder,
did little Goddie Mumford play *mum*blety-peg with it?"

At this terminal extravagance—this spacecraft leap into
whimsy—the Chief could not avoid a groan. Ellery rose, un-
dismayed.

"It's that kind of case, Newby. And by the way, there's one
line of investigation I haven't followed through yet. The
search for that safe combination sidetracked me. I'll look into
it tomorrow morning."

*   *   *

January 12: Having strained his prerogatives as a
houseguest by arranging to borrow one of the Mumford cars,
Ellery came downstairs the next morning before anyone else
was up; and as he was passing the table in the foyer something caught his eye. There was a letter on the silver salver.

Being the world's nosiest noonan, Mr. Q paused to look it
over. The dime-store envelope was unstamped, unpost-
marked, and addressed in a childishly disguised scrawl.

The envelope read: *To Ellery.*

He was surprised and delighted—surprised because the letter was so totally unexpected, delighted because he was in
great need of a new point of inquiry. He tore open the envelope and removed from it a sheet of cheap notepaper.

The handwriting of the message was similarly disguised:

12/1/65
Mum's the word. If you tell what you know I'll kill you,
too.

There was no signature.

Was this a new development? Hardly. All it did was obfus-
cate the mystification. The letter was from a not too uncom-
mon type—the garrulous murderer; but what was he, Ellery,
supposed to "know"? Whatever it was, he ardently wished he
knew it.

He began to chew on the problem. After a while he began
to look more cheerful. Obviously, his supposed knowledge
was dangerous to the murderer. A yeast was therefore at
work in the brew. Fear—the killer's fear—might produce a
viscid potion on which the killer would choke.

Ellery slipped the letter into his pocket and left the house.

He drove the station wagon to Connhaven, where he made
for the Merrimac campus. Here he sought out the university
museum. In the main office of the tomblike building he found
waiting for him—he had telephoned ahead for the appointment—Wolcott Thorp.

"You have me all atwitter, Mr. Queen." The curator
touched Ellery's hand with his papery paw. "And not entirely
at ease. I assume you're working on poor Godfrey's murder.
Why me?"

"You're a suspect," Ellery pointed out.

"Of course!" And Thorp hastened to add, "Aren't we all?
If I'm acting guilty, it's human nature."

"That's the trouble, or one of them." Ellery smiled. "I'm
familiar with the psychology of guilt by confrontation, even
of the innocent. But that's not what I'm here for, so stop

worrying. A museum to me is what the circus is to small boys. Do you have time to show me around yours?"

"Oh, yes!" Thorp began to beam.

"I'm curious about your particular field. It's West Africa, isn't it?"

The beam became sheer sunshine. "My friend," said Wolcott Thorp, "come with me! No, this way . . ."

For the next hour Ellery was the beneficiary of the man's genuine erudition. Ellery's interest was by no means simulated. He had a deep-rooted feeling for antiquity and anthropology (what was it but detection of a different kind?), and he was fascinated by the artifacts Thorp showed him from what had been western Sudan and the district of Kayes on the Senegal—idols and tutelary gods, fetishes, masks, charms, headdresses of pompons used by the Mandingos to ward off the powers of evil.

Happily inundated with the information, Ellery finally interrupted the curator's flow long enough to ask for a sheet of paper on which to make notes. The curator obliged with a piece of museum stationery; and Ellery, preparing to notate, forced himself back from the dark tribalisms of Africa.

The inscription on the museum letterhead was arranged in two lines. The top line was simply the initials of the museum; the line below spelled out the full name: Merrimac University Museum.

The top line . . . MUM.

Thorp had excused himself for a moment; and folding the paper, clean of unnoted notes, Ellery took from his pocket the anonymous letter he had picked up from the salver that morning. He was about to insert the museum letterhead into the envelope when his attention was caught by the envelope's scrawled salutation.

To Ellery.

No, that was wrong!

To was correct enough, as he had read it, but not *Ellery.* The final letter had a long tail on it; this tail had been the cause of his mistaken reading. On re-examination the *ry* was not an *ry* at all; it was a straggle-tailed *n.*

To Ellen.

It was Ellen who knew something dangerous to the killer.

It was Ellen who was being threatened.

Wolcott Thorp, returning, was astounded to see his visitor clap a hand to his head, jam a letter into his pocket, and dart out without so much as a fare-thee-well.

Crouched over the wheel of the station wagon, Ellery

roared back to Wrightsville and the Mumford house, cursing
every impediment that forced him to slacken speed. He left
the car in the driveway and clattered past an alarmed Margaret Caswell and up the stairs in the longest leaps his long
legs could manage.

He burst into Ellen's room.

Ellen, proped up on a chaise longue by a picture window
in some flowing garment that might have been designed for a
painting by Gainsborough, was sipping hot chocolate from
what could only have been—even in his agitation Ellery noticed it—a bone-china mustache cup.

"Am I supposed to be flattered, Mr. Queen," asked Ellen
in a her-Ladyship-is-not-amused sort of voice, "by your boor-
ish intrusion?"

"Beg pardon," panted Ellery. "I thought you might be
dead."

Her Wedgewood eyes blued further. She set the antique
cup down on an end table. "Did you say *dead?*"

He extended the anonymous letter. "Read this."

"What is it?"

"It's for you. I found it on the salver this morning and
opened it by mistake, thinking it was addressed to me. I'm
thankful I did. And you may be, too, before we're finished."

She took the letter and read it swiftly. The paper slipped
from her hand, struck the edge of the chaise, and fluttered to
the floor.

"What does it mean?" she whispered. "I don't understand."

"I think you do." Ellery stooped over her. "You know
something dangerous to your father's murderer, and your father's murderer knows you know it. Ellen, tell me what it is,
for the sake of your own safety. Think! What do you know
that would explain a threat like this?"

He read in her eyes the immediate qualification of her terror. A slyness crept into them, and the lids slid halfway
down.

"I don't know what you're talking about."

"It's foolhardy of you to hold it back. We have a murderer
on our hands and he's getting edgy. Tell me, Ellen."

"There's nothing to tell. I know nothing." She turned
away. "Now will you please leave? I'm not exactly dressed
for entertaining."

Ellery retrieved the note and left, damning all idiots. In ad-
dition to his other commitments he would now have to un-
dertake the thankless task of acting as the woman's watch-
dog.

What was Ellen concealing?

*   *   *

Christopher, sighting the pale sun over the top of a pine, recited the opening lines of *Snowbound*.

"Whittier," he explained. "I still have a childish fondness for the old boy."

Joanne laughed, a sound of sleigh bells. "Delivered like a pro. Bravo."

"Not really. A pro gets fairly steady employment."

"You could, too, if you tried. Really tried."

"You think so?"

"I know so."

"You know something? So do I. But only when I'm with you."

"I'm glad."

"Enough to cleave to my bosom?"

"I don't quite know," said Joanne cautiously, "how to take that, Chris."

"Take it as an interim proposal. I don't want to tie you up in knots until I've made it all the way. You make me feel life-size, Jo. I suppose what I'm trying to say is that I need you."

Jo smiled, but inside. She slipped a little mittened hand into his glove, and they strolled toward the pines and the pale sun.

Wolcott Thorp came down from the university and Chief Newby drove over from headquarters after dinner, both at Ellery's invitation.

"What's up?" Newby asked Ellery, aside. "Have you come up with something?"

"Have you?" asked Ellery.

"Not a damn thing. I'm not the Wizard of Oz, the way you're supposed to be. No miracles yet?"

"No miracles, I'm afraid."

"Then what's cooking tonight?"

"A mess. I'm going to fling it at them, and see who runs for the mop—if any."

They joined the others in the drawing room.

"I've taken the liberty of asking Chief Newby to drop by," Ellery began, "because we need, I think, to redefine our position. Especially in reference to the dying message.

"When Chief Newby and I first found M-U-M on the scene, we made the natural assumption that Godfrey Mumford had left it as a clue to his killer's identity. Further thought compromised this theory, at least as far as I was concerned. The clue had so many possible interpretations that I shifted to the theory that meant the safe combination. That worked out fine but accomplished nothing. I opened the safe, and the safe proved to be empty."

Ellery paused, seeming to wing far off. But his vision was in focus, and he could see nothing in their faces but attentiveness and bafflement.

"Now, after thinking it over again, I've changed my mind again," he went on. "If Godfrey had wanted to leave the combination, all he had to write down was 13-21-13. It would have been almost as easy to write as M-U-M, and there would have been no chance of its being misunderstood. So now I've gone back to the original theory, which Newby has never abandoned—namely, that the message points to the murderer's identity. If so, to whom?"

He paused again; and most of his captive audience waited in varying stages of nervousness for revelation.

"The Chief," said Ellery, with a side glance at Mrs. Caswell, who alone seemed unmoved, "is convinced of that identity. And, of course, from a strictly logical point of view, it is certainly possible."

"It is certainly *stuff*," said Mum; then pulled her head back in like a turtle.

"If it's stuff, Mrs. Caswell," smiled Ellery, "what's coming is pure moonshine. Yet—who knows? I'm not going to turn my back on a theory simply because it sounds like something out of Lewis Carroll. Bear with me.

"From the beginning this case has exhibited a remarkable series of what I have to call, for want of a more elegant term, 'doubles.'

"For example, there have been at least four 'doubles' connected with the murdered man: Godfrey had developed a famous chrysanthemum with a *double* blossom on one stem; the party he gave was to celebrate a *double* event, New Year's Eve and his seventieth birthday; his wall safe cost about *double* what it should have cost; and his children, Ellen and Christopher, are twins—another *double*.

"Further, let's not overlook the most significant *double* in the case: the double mystery of who killed Godfrey and what happened to the Imperial Pendant.

"What's more, we can go on through a great many more doubles. Because, if you interpret the dying message as a clue to the killer, each of you has at least two connections with MUM.

"For instance, Ellen." Ellen gave a visible start. "One, her maiden name was Mumford—first syllable, *Mum*. Second,

she's married to an Egyptologist. Egyptology connotes pyr-
amids, the Sphinx—and *mum*mies."

Ellen reacted with a double sort of sound, like a jeer
crossed with a neigh. "Rubbish! Nonsense!"

"It is, isn't it? Yet this thing gets curiouser and curiouser.
Take Christopher. Again, the first syllable of *Mum*ford. And
second, Chris, your profession."

"My profession?" asked Christopher, puzzled. "I'm an
actor."

"And what are other words for actor? Player, performer,
thespian, trouper . . . *mum*mer."

Christopher's handsome face reddened; he seemed torn between the impulse to laugh and the need to fume. As a com-
promise he simply threw up his hands.

Chief Newby was looking embarrassed. "Are you serious,
Ellery?"

"Why, I don't know whether I am or not," said Ellery
gravely. "I'm just trying it on for size. You're next, Mr.
Thorp."

The elderly curator immediately looked frightened. "I?
How do I fit in?"

"First, the initials of the museum as they appear on your
stationery: Merrimac University Museum—M-U-M. Second,
your special interest in the culture of West Africa and its artifacts: fetishes, masks, charms, talismans—oh, and pompons."

"I fail," said Thorp coldly, "to see the connection."

"The pompon is a variety of chrysanthe*mum*. And if you
want still another cross-reference, Mr. Thorp, there's a phrase
to describe your special field. Surely you know it?"

Here Thorp's erudition was apparently wanting. He shook
his head.

"*Mum*bo jumbo," Ellery solemnly told him.

Thorp looked astonished. Then he chuckled. "How true. In
fact, the very words come from the language of the Klas-
sonke, a Mandingo tribe. What a quaint coincidence!"

"Yes," said Ellery; and the way he said it re-established the
mood the museum man's laughter was shattering. "And Mrs.
Caswell. I remind you again that Chief Newby has all along
thought the dying message points to you. *Mum* Caswell."

Margaret Caswell's features took on the slightest pallor. "I
hardly think this is the time to be playing games, Mr. Queen.
But—all right, I'll play, too. You said that each of us has at
least two connections with Godfrey's word on that pad.
What's the other one of mine?"

Ellery's tone was positively apologetic. "I've noticed that

you're fond of beer, Mrs. Caswell, particularly German beer. One of the best known of the German beers is called *mum*."

And this at last brought Joanne to her feet, her little hands clenched. Her anger gave her a charming dimension.

"At first this was plain ridiculous," stormed Jo. "Now it's —it's criminally asinine! Are you purposely making fun of us? And if I may ask a silly question—and no doubt I'll get a pair of silly answers—what are *my* two connections with MUM?"

"There," mourned Ellery, "you have me, Jo. I haven't been able to spot one connection, let alone two."

"Quite amusing, I'm sure," Ellen said. "Meanwhile, we're neglecting the important thing. What happened to the pendant?"

All Christopher's dissatisfaction with the Queen performance burst out at finding a target he felt free to attack. *"Important* thing," he cried. "I can't make head or tail of what's going on here, but don't you consider it important to find out who killed father, Ellen? Aren't you concerned with anything but that damned pendant? You make me feel like a ghoul!"

"Don't flatter yourself," Ellen said to her twin. "You're nothing so impressive as a ghoul, Chris. What you are is a bloody ass."

He turned his back on his sister; and regal as a Borgia, she stalked from the room. From the stairway her complaint came to them distinctly: "You'd think father would have installed a lift instead of making us climb these antediluvian stairs."

"Yes, your Majesty!" yelled Christopher.

While Mr. Q murmured to Chief Newby, "Ellery in Blunderland. Through the Magnifying Glass . . ."

"What are you," snarled the Chief of Police, grabbing his coat and hat, "a nut or something?"

January 13: The one morning of the week when Ellen could be relied on to come down for breakfast was Sunday. Invariably she descended to a kipper and a slice of dry toast (except on communion days), after which, trailing High Church clouds of glory, she strode off to join her Anglican co-worshipers.

It was therefore a matter of remark that on this particular Sunday morning she failed to appear.

It was especially remarkable to Ellery, who had been barred by the proprieties from passing the night guarding her bedside. Enlisting Margaret Caswell's chaperonage, he rushed upstairs, kicked open the unlocked door, and dashed in.

Ellen was still in bed. He listened frantically to her breathing; he took her pulse; he shook her, shouting in her ear. Then he damned her perversity and the unlocked door, which was an example of it.

"Phone Conk Farnham!" he bellowed at Mrs. Caswell.

There followed a scene of chaos, not without its absurdity, like an old Mac Sennett comedy. Its climax came when, for the umpteenth time in ten days, Dr. Farnham arrived on the run with his little black bag. It was surely Conk's opinion, thought Ellery, that he was hopelessly trapped in the antics of a houseful of lunatics.

"Sleeping pills," the doctor said. "Slight overdose. No need for treatment; she didn't take enough. She'll come out of it by herself soon—in fact, she's coming out of it now."

"This must be it on the night table," Ellery mumbled.

"What?"

"The medium of the pills."

A cup of scummy cold chocolate sat there, almost full.

"That's it, all right," said Dr. Farnham, after touching the tip of his tongue to it. "It's loaded. If she'd swallowed the whole cupful, Ellery, she'd have been done for."

"When will she be able to talk?"

"As soon as she's all the way out."

Ellery snapped his fingers. "Excuse me, Conk!" he said, and dashed past Mrs. Caswell and tore down the stairs. In the breakfast room, silent and glum, sat Jo and Chris and Wolcott Thorp.

"How's Ellen?" Chris asked, half rising.

"Sit down. She's all right. This time. Now we can start worrying about next time."

"Next time?"

"Somebody slipped a lethal overdose of sleeping pills in her hot chocolate before she went to bed last night—unless you're prepared to argue that Ellen is the type who would attempt suicide, which in my book she definitely is not. Anyway, she took only a few sips, thereby surviving. But whoever tried to kill her may try another time, and my guess is the time will be sooner rather than later. So let's not dawdle. Who knows who prepared the hot chocolate last night?"

"I do," said Joanne. "She prepared it herself. I was in the kitchen with her."

"All the time she was fixing it?"

"No, I left before she did."

"Anyone else in the kitchen at the time, or near it?"

"Not I," said Christopher promptly, wiping his brow, which for some reason was damp. "If I ever give way to one of my homicidal impulses toward Ellen, I'll use something sure like cyanide."

But no one smiled.

"You, Mr. Thorp?" asked Ellery, fixing the curator with a glittering eye.

"Not I," said the little man, stuttering.

"Had anyone gone up to bed?"

"I don't think so," said Jo, her eyes worried. "No, I'm sure no one had. It was just after we finished that crazy farce of yours in the drawing room—when Ellen pranced out, I mean. A few minutes later she came downstairs again to prepare her chocolate. All the rest of us were still here. Don't you remember?"

"No, because I was seeing Chief Newby out, and we talked outside for a few minutes before he drove off. Unfortunately I share the general weakness of being unable to be in two places at the same time. Did Ellen go directly upstairs with her chocolate?"

"I can answer that," said Christopher. "I'd gone to the library to lick my wounds, and Ellen came in for a book to read in bed, she said. She wasn't there more than two or three minutes. She took one of yours, if I'm not mistaken."

"Maybe that's why she fell asleep so soon," said Jo with a little snap-crackle-pop in her voice.

"Even that," said Ellery with a bow, "is not impossible. In any event, she must have left her cup standing in the kitchen for those two or three minutes."

"I guess so," said Christopher. "It would also seem that we were all milling around, with opportunity to dodge into the kitchen and tamper with it, allowing for a healthy lie or two. Take your pick, Mr. Queen. In my own defense I can only say I didn't do it."

"Nor," stuttered little Wolcott Thorp, "did I."

"It looks," said Jo, "as if you'll have to make the most of what you have."

"Which," snapped Ellery, "is precious little."

And he left them to go back upstairs, where he found Dr. Farnham preparing to depart. Ellen was awake, propped up against the headboard, looking not hung over at all. What she did look was hostile and furtive.

Ellery went to work.

But his most tried techniques, running from the sympathetic plea to the horrendous warning, failed to budge her. Her brush with death seemed to have left her only the more doggedly crouched over whatever secret she was concealing. The most Ellery could pry out of her was the admission that she had bought sleeping pills herself from a local "chemist," on the prescription of another doctor in town whom she did not name. Finally, slipping down in the bed, she turned her face to the wall and refused to answer any more of his questions whatsoever.

Checkmated, Ellery withdrew, leaving Mrs. Caswell on guard.

Someone else, he thought, was at the moment sharing his frustration. The agent of the sleeping pills.

The dinner conversation had gaps. Ellery pushed the food around on his plate. Ellen attempted a show of Empire fortitude, but the attempt was sorry, and he suspected that she had come down to the dinner table only because of the creepy isolation of her bedroom.

Margaret Caswell sat in a tense posture that suggested listening, as for the baying of bloodhounds. Christopher and Joanne sought reassurance in eloquent eye examination of each other. Wolcott Thorp tried to stimulate a discussion of some recent Fulah acquisitions by the museum, but no one listened even politely, and he too fell under the spell of the pervasive gloom.

They were about to leave the dinner table when the doorbell rang with an angry chime. Ellery leaped to life.

"Chief Newby," he said. "I'll let him in, if no one minds. Please go to the drawing room—all of you. We're going to get on with this lethal nonsense and make something of it if it takes all night."

He hurried to the front door. Newby hurled his hat and overcoat on a tapestried chair but pointedly failed to remove his overshoes, as if announcing that at the first sound of jabberwocky he intended to exit.

They joined the others in the drawing room, and Newby said, "All right, Ellery, get on with it."

"Let's begin," Ellery said, "with a fact. The fact that you, Ellen, are in imminent danger. What we don't know, and must know, is why. It's something only you can tell us, and I suggest you do so before it's too late. I remind you that the murderer of your father is here in this room, listening and watching."

Four pairs of eyes shifted from Ellen immediately, but they came right back again.

Ellen's lips remained drawn down at the corners, like a scar. "I told you—I don't know what you're talking about."

"You're afraid, of course. But do you think you're going to buy immunity with silence? A murderer needs to sleep at night, too, and his best assurance of peace of mind is your permanent removal. So talk while you still can."

"It's my job to warn you, Mrs. Nash," Chief Newby put in sourly, "that if you're holding back evidence, you're committing a crime. How much trouble do you want to be in?"

But Ellen fixed her eyes on the fists in her lap.

"All right," said Ellery, and his tone was so odd that even Ellen stirred. "If you won't talk, I will.

"Let's start all over again. What did Godfrey mean by writing M-U-M? Ignore what I've said before about it. I've now come to a final conclusion.

"A man clear-headed enough to leave a dying message is clear-headed enough to avoid ambiguity. Since MUM involved most of you—and in more ways than one, farfetched as most of them are—then I have to conclude that Godfrey did not intend MUM to indicate the identity of his murderer.

"Consequently, once more I have to go back to what Godfrey did promise to leave you—the combination of his safe."

"But you went through all that," exploded Newby. "And it washed out—the safe was empty."

"Not a complete washout, Newby. I translated MUM into numbers because of the twenty-six numbers on the dial, and that proved correct as far as it went. But what if it didn't go far enough? Remember the doubles? One was that the safe cost Godfrey about double what it should have. *What if there was a good, solid, practical reason for that double cost?* Suppose there's more to that safe than meets the eye—*some feature that cost the extra money.* Double cost . . . *how about double safe?*"

That brought their mouths open, and he continued swiftly. "If it was a double safe, there would be *two* combinations. One would work by the numbers 13-21-13, as it does, and would open the orthodox safe. The other combination would open another safe!—which obviously must be contained *within* the safe, making an inner, smaller safe. And suppose —since that's the word Godfrey wrote down just before he died—suppose that not only is MUM the combination for the outer safe, but MUM is also the combination for the inner safe. One MUM translating into numbers, the second remaining exactly what it is—*a word of three letters.*"

"But there aren't any letters on the dial," protested Newby.

"Right. But remember what's etched on the rim of the knob? The name and address of the manufacturer: VULCAN SAFE & LOCK COMPANY, INC. NEW HAVEN, CONN. And you'll note that, contained in those words, are an M and a U!

"Shall we try it?"

Ellery went over to the oil painting and slid it to one side. He revolved the dial a few times, then turned it until the M of COMPANY lay directly under the alignment notch; then he turned right to the U of VULCAN, aligning that, then left back to the M of COMPANY.

He pulled on the knob.

The safe door did not swing open. Instead, the knob came out in his hand! And behind the knob, within the thickness of the safe door, where the tumblers and mechanism lay, appeared a small compartment—a safe within a safe. And in the compartment, flashing like a minor sun surrounded by sixteen glowing planets, was the Imperial Pendant.

"Alagazam," Ellery said softly, holding it aloft so that the light from the old-fashioned crystal chandelier blazed from the pendant in a thousand coruscations. "When Mr. Mumford put the necklace away, his back must have been to you, and it was a broad back. It was into the knob-safe that he put this, not into the regular one. That's why he probably never bothered to put the pendant in a bank vault, Christopher. Even if someone tried to burgle this safe, could he dream that the real safe was behind the knob? It was, if you'll excuse the pun, very safe indeed. Here, Newby, I imagine you'd better take charge of this until the will is probated and certain other matters are cleared up."

And Ellery tossed the pendant to Newby, while the others' heads moved in unison, like the heads of spectators at a tennis match.

"Q.E.D.," said Ellery. "One half of our mystery is solved. It remains only to solve the other half.

"Who killed Godfrey Mumford?"

He faced them with such fierceness that they all shrank back.

"I've known since yesterday morning who the murderer is," Ellery said. "There wasn't a chance, by the way, that he'd take off—not so long as the pendant was missing. It was the finding of the pendant that was holding me up, too.

"I want you all to look at this letter from the murderer to Ellen. Examine it carefully."

He took it from his pocket and handed it to Chief Newby, who looked it over, scowled, and passed it on.

12/1/65

Mum's the word. If you tell what you know I'll kill you, too.

When it came back to him from Thorp, the last to read it, Ellery could detect nothing but blankness on any face.

"You don't see it?"

"Come on, Ellery," Newby rasped. "So I'm as blind as the rest and you've got the eyes of a chicken hawk. What's the point?"

"The point is the date."

"The date?"

"The date at the top. *12/1/65.*"

"Why, that's wrong," said Jo suddenly. "It's January, not December."

"Correct. The letter was left on the salver the morning of January twelfth—*1/12/65*. The writer reversed the numerals for the month and day. Why? In the United States we write the month numeral first, always, *then* the day numeral. *It's in England that they do it the opposite way.*

"Who in this household has been living in England for years? Who uses the Anglicism 'trunk call' for 'long distance'? Who says 'lift' for 'elevator,' 'Chief Constable' for 'Chief of Police,' 'chemist' instead of 'druggist' or 'pharmacist'?

"Ellen, of course. Ellen, who wrote this 'threatening' letter to herself."

Ellen was glaring at Ellery as if he had turned into a monster from outer space. "No! I didn't!"

But Ellery ignored her. "And why should Ellen have written a threatening letter to herself? Well, what was the effect the letter produced? It made her look as though she were next in line to be murdered—by implication, therefore, innocent of killing Godfrey.

"This was doubly indicated by the clumsy poisoning attempt on herself—an evident phony. She never meant to drink more than a few sips. The whole hot chocolate episode was designed to make that 'threat' look good."

Now his eyes found Ellen's and locked.

"Why should you want to make yourself look innocent, Ellen? The innocent don't have to *make* themselves look innocent. Only the guilty—"

"Are you accusing *me?*" Ellen shrieked. "Of stabbing my own father to death?" She looked about wildly. "Chris, Jo—you can't believe—*Mum!*"

But Ellery drove ahead without mercy. "The clue points directly to you, Ellen, and only to you. Of course, if you've anything to say that puts a different complexion on all this, I advise you to say it now."

Ellery kept her gaze pinned down like a butterfly specimen. She began to tremble. And as she did so, he suddenly said in the kindest of voices, "Don't be afraid any more,

Ellen. You see, I know what you know. All I want you to do is to speak out, to tell us what you know."

And she did, her story rushing out. "I was up the night father was murdered—couldn't sleep for some reason. It was long past midnight. While I was in the upstairs hall, on my way down to the kitchen for a snack . . . I happened to see somebody sneak out of father's room. I was sure he saw me. I was afraid to tell . . ."

"And who was it you saw, Ellen?"

"It was . . . it was . . ." And her arm shot out—". . . it was Wolcott Thorp!"

Ellery went early to his room, packed his suitcases, and slipped like the Arab silently away, leaving behind a bread-and-butter note. He did not check back in to the Hollis, the savor having for now gone out of Wrightsville; but he had a couple of hours to kill before plane time, and he killed them, appropriately, at police headquarters.

"Ellery!" Chief Newby greeted him, rising and seizing his hand. "I was hoping you'd drop in. I never did get to thank you properly. That was a slick scene you put on last night. You told a real whopper."

"I may have told," said Ellery soberly, "several."

"You said you knew what Ellen knew."

"Oh, that. Yes, of course. But I had to get her to talk; I was reasonably certain that was what she was holding back. And that letter business—"

"Did you really think she wrote that letter?"

"Not for a moment. Except for psychos, murderers don't admit their killings—even in disguised handwritings—at a time when they're not even suspected. And Ellen's Britishness was so blatant that anyone could have used the British dating system to frame her. So although I knew she hadn't written that threatening letter to herself, I accused her of it last night to frighten her into putting the finger on Thorp.

"Thorp, of course, was the one who wrote the letter. He counted on my spotting the Anglicism and pinning it on Ellen for the reason I gave—that double whammy about if-she-wants-us-to-think-she's-innocent-she-must-be-guilty. And if I hadn't spotted it, he could always have called it to my attention.

"It may even be that Thorp originally designed the frame-up letter to be used by him in the event Ellen did talk and accused him of what she'd seen. The trouble was, even when Ellen kept her mouth shut, Thorp had second thoughts. That poisoned chocolate business wasn't an attempt on Ellen's part to make herself look innocent, as I mendaciously suggested last night in putting the pressure on her; it was a genuine attempt by Thorp to shut her mouth before she could open it. He expected us—if it had succeeded—to accept it as a suicide-confession."

"Incidentally," said the Chief, "you said you knew it was Thorp—"

"A slight exaggeration. I had reason to suspect Thorp, but I had no proof—not an iota; and I was afraid another attack on Ellen might succeed."

"But why," asked the Chief, "would a man like Thorp murder his best friend in cold blood? He's confessed to the killing, but we haven't been able to get a word out of him about motive. It certainly can't be that measly twenty thousand Godfrey was leaving him."

Ellery sighed. "The collector breed are a strange lot, Newby. In spite of what he told Godfrey, Thorp probably didn't consider himself too old to go on that expedition to West Africa; he must have been waiting desperately for years for what he thought was going to be a hundred thousand dollars to finance the trip. When he learned that Godfrey's carelessness had caused it to shrink to only one-fifth of that, he flipped. That expedition was the dream of his life. Is there anyone we can come to hate more than the loved one who disappoints and frustrates us?"

Newby held up his hand as Ellery rose. "Wait a minute! What made you suspect Thorp in the first place? It must be something fancy I missed."

Ellery did not display pride. His Wrightsville triumphs too often felt like defeats. Perhaps it was because he loved the old town, and it had been his lot to clean up her filth.

"Nothing fancy, Newby. The dreariest kind of slip on Thorp's part. When you and I first went to the house, they told us in detail what had gone on at the discovery of the body. The line of previous action was very clear. Margaret Caswell rushed out of Godfrey's bedroom, crying out that the old man was—mark the word—*dead*. They all rushed upstairs except Thorp, who went to the downstairs phone, called Dr. Farnham, then called you here at headquarters. And what did Thorp tell you? That Mumford had been found, not merely dead, but *murdered*. Why should Thorp have leaped to the conclusion that the old man's death was unnatural *unless he already knew it?*

"You know, Newby," Ellery said with a half smile that apologized in advance, "Wolcott Thorp would have been far, far better off if he'd followed his own advice and—forgive me—kept mum."

CONTEMPORARY PROBLEMS IN DEDUCTION

Object Lesson

Ellery hurried down West 92nd Street toward the main entrance of Henry Hudson High School stealing guilty glances at his watch. Miss Carpenter had been crisply specific about place, date, and time: her home room, 109; Friday morning, April 22nd; first period ("Bell *at 8:40*, Mr. Queen"). Miss Carpenter, who had come to him with an unusual request, had struck him as the sort of dedicated young person who would not take kindly to a hitch in her crusade.

Ellery broke into an undignified lope.

The project for which she had enlisted his aid was formidable even for a crusading young teacher of Social Studies on the 9th Grade Junior High level. For two months merchants of the neighborhood had been reporting stores broken into by a teen-age gang. Beyond establishing that the crimes were the work of the same boys, who were probably students at Henry Hudson High School, the police had got nowhere.

Miss Carpenter, walking home from a movie late the previous Monday night, had seen three boys dive out of a smashed bakery window and vanish into an alley. She had recognized them as Howard Ruffo, David Strager, and Joey Buell, all 15-year-old home-room students of hers. The juvenile crime problem was solved.

But not for Miss Carpenter. Instead of going to the police, Miss Carpenter had gone to Ellery, who lived on West 87th Street and was a hero to the youth of the neighborhood. Howard, David, and Joey were *not* hardened delinquents, she had told him, and she could *not* see their arrest, trial, and imprisonment as a solution to anything. True, they had substituted gang loyalty for the love and security they were denied

49

in their unhappy slum homes, but boys who worked at after-school jobs and turned every cent in at home were hardly beyond recall, were they? And she had told him just where each boy worked, and at what.

"They're only patterning their behavior after criminals because they think criminals are strong, successful, and glamorous," Miss Carpenter had said; and what she would like him to do was visit her class and, under the pretext of giving a talk on the subject of Notorious Criminals I Have Known, paint such a picture of weak, ratting, empty, and violently ending criminality that David and Joey and Howard would see the error of their ways.

It had seemed to Ellery that this placed a rather hefty burden on his oratorical powers. Did Miss Carpenter have her principal's permission for this project?

No, Miss Carpenter had replied bravely, she did *not* have Mr. Hinsdale's permission, and she might very well lose her job when he heard about it. "But I'm *not* going to be the one who gives those boys the first shove toward reform school and maybe eventually a life sentence!" And besides, what did Mr. Queen have to lose but an hour of his time?

So Mr. Queen had feebly said yes, he would come; and here he was, at the door of the determined young woman's classroom . . . seven minutes *late*.

Ellery braced himself and opened the door.

The moment he set foot in the room he knew he had walked in on a catastrophe.

Louise Carpenter stood tensely straight at her desk, her pretty face almost as white as the envelope she was clutching. And she was glaring at a mass of boy and girl faces so blankly, so furtively quiet that the silence sizzled.

The first thing she said to him was, "I've been robbed."

The terrible mass of boy and girl eyes followed him to her desk. In his nose was the pungent smell of ink, glue, paper, chalk, musty wardrobe closets; surrounding him were discolored walls, peeling paint, tarnished fixtures, warped window poles and mutilated desks.

"Robbed in my own classroom," Miss Carpenter choked.

He laid his coat and hat gently on her desk. "A practical joke?" He smiled at the class.

"Hardly. They didn't know you were coming." They had betrayed her, the sick shock in her voice said. "Class, this is Ellery Queen. I don't have to tell you who Mr. Queen is, and how honored we are to have him visit us." There was a gasp, a buzz, a spatter of applause. "Mr. Queen was kind enough to come here today as a special treat to give us a talk on crime. I didn't know he was going to walk in on one."

The spatter stopped dead.

"You're sure there has been a crime, Miss Carpenter?"

"An envelope with seven one-dollar bills in it was stolen, and from the way it happened the thief can only be someone in this room."

"I'm sorry to hear that."

He deliberately looked them over, wondering which of the forty-one pairs of eyes staring back at his belonged to Joey Buell, Howard Ruffo, and David Strager. He should have asked Louise Carpenter to describe them. Now it was too late.

Or was it?

It seemed to Ellery that three of the twenty-odd boy faces were rather too elaborately blank. One of them was set on husky shoulders; this boy was blond, handsome, and dead-white about the nostrils. The second was a sharp-nosed, jet-haired boy with Mediterranean coloring who was perfectly still except for his fingers, and they kept turning a pencil over and over almost ritually. The third, thin and red-haired, showed no life anywhere except in a frightened artery in his temple.

Ellery made up his mind.

"Well, if it's a real live crime," he said, turning to Louise, "I don't imagine anyone wants to hear me ramble on about crimes that are dead and buried. In fact, I think it would be more interesting if I gave the class a demonstration of how a crime is actually solved. What do you think, Miss Carpenter?"

Understanding leaped into her eyes, along with hope.

"I think," she said grimly, "it would be *lots* more interesting."

"Suppose we begin by finding out about the seven dollars. They were yours, Miss Carpenter?"

"One dollar was mine. Miss McDoud, an English teacher, is being married next month. A group of us are chipping in to buy her a wedding present, with me as banker. All this week teachers have been dropping in to leave their dollars in an envelope I've had on my desk. This morning—"

"That's fine for background, Miss Carpenter. Suppose we hear testimony from the class." Ellery surveyed them, and there was a ripple of tittering. Suddenly he pointed to a little lipsticked girl with an Italian haircut. "Would you like to tell us what happened this morning?"

"I don't know anything about the money!"

"Chicken." A boy's jeering voice.

"The boy who said that." Ellery kept his tone friendly. It was one of the three he had spotted, the husky blond one. "What's your name?"

"David Strager." His sneer said, *You don't scare me.* But his nostrils remained dead-white. He was the boy Miss Carpenter had said worked after school as a stock boy at the Hi-Kwality Supermarket on Amsterdam Avenue.

"All right, Dave. You tell us about this morning."

The boy glanced scornfully at the girl with the Italian haircut. "We all knew the money was in the envelope. This morning before the bell rings Mrs. Morrell comes in with her buck and Miss Carpenter puts it with the other money and lays the envelope on her desk. So afterward the bell rings, Mrs. Morrell splits, Miss Carpenter picks up the envelope and takes a look inside, and she hollers, 'I been robbed.'"

The thin boy with the red hair called out, "So what are we supposed to do, drop dead?" and winked at David Strager, who had already sat down. The big blond boy winked back.

"And your name?" Ellery asked the redhead.

"Joseph Buell," the boy answered defiantly. He was the one who worked at Kaplan's, the big cigar, candy, and stationery store on 89th Street. "Who wants their old seven bucks?"

"Somebody not only wants it, Joey, somebody's got it."

"Aaa, for all we know she took it herself." And this was the third of the trio, the sharp-faced dark boy. If Ellery was right, he was the one who delivered part-time for O'Donnel's Dry Cleaning on Columbus Avenue.

"And you are—?"

"Howard Ruffo."

The Three Musketeers, rushing to one another's support.

"You mean, Howard, you're charging Miss Carpenter with having stolen the teachers' money?" Ellery asked with a smile.

The boy's dark glance wavered. "I mean maybe she took it like by mistake. Mislaid it or somepin'."

"As a matter of fact," came Louise's quiet voice, "when I saw the money wasn't in the envelope, my first thought was exactly that, Mr. Queen. So I searched myself thoroughly."

"May I see the envelope?"

"This isn't the one I was keeping the seven dollars in"— she handed him the envelope—"though it looks the same. I have a box of them in my locker there. The lock hasn't worked for ages. This one must have been stolen from my locker yesterday, or earlier this week."

"It's a blank envelope, Miss Carpenter. How do you know it isn't the one that contained the money?"

"Because the original had a notation in ink on the flap—*Gift Fund for Helen McDoud*." She looked about and glances fell in windrows. "So this theft was planned, Mr. Queen. Someone came to class this morning armed with this duplicate envelope, previously stolen and filled with worthless paper, prepared to make a quick exchange if the opportunity arose. And it did. The class was milling around while Mrs. Morrell and I chatted."

The paper in the substitute envelope consisted of a sheaf of rectangular strips cut to the size of dollar bills.

"At the time you placed Mrs. Morrell's dollar among the others in the original envelope, was everybody here?"

"Yes. The door opened and closed only once after that—when Mrs. Morrell left. I was facing the door the whole time."

"Could Mrs. Morrell, as a practical joke, have made the switch?"

"She wasn't anywhere near my desk after I laid the envelope on it."

"Then you're right, Miss Carpenter. The theft was planned in advance by one of the boys or girls in this room, and the thief—and money—are both still here."

The tension was building beautifully. The boy must be in a sweat. He hadn't expected his theft to be found out so soon, before he got a chance to sneak the money out of the room.

"What time does the first period end, Miss Carpenter?"

"At 9:35."

Every head turned toward the clock on the wall.

"And it's only 8:56," Ellery said cheerfully. "That gives us thirty-nine minutes—more than enough time. Unless the boy or girl who planned this crime wants to return the loot to Miss Carpenter here and now?"

This time he stared directly from David to Howard to Joey. His stare said, *I hate to do this, boys, but of course I'll have to if you think you can get away with it.*

The Strager boy's full lips were twisted. The skinny red-head, Joey Buell, stared back sullenly. Howard Ruffo's pencil twirled faster.

It's one of those three, all right.

"I see we'll have to do it the hard way," Ellery said. "Sorry I can't produce the thief with a flick of my wrist, the way it's done in books, but in real life detection—like crime—is pretty unexciting stuff. We'll begin with a body search. It's voluntary, by the way. Anybody rather not chance a search? Raise your hand."

Not a muscle moved.

"I'll search the boys, Miss Carpenter. You roll those two bulletin boards over to that corner and search the girls."

The next few minutes were noisy. As each boy was searched and released he was sent to the blackboard at the front of the room. The girls were sent to the rear.

"Find anything, Miss Carpenter?"

"Rose Perez has a single dollar bill. The other girls either have small change or no money at all."

"No sign of the original envelope?"

"No."

"I found two boys with bills—in each case a single, too. David Strager and Joey Buell. No envelope."

Louise's brows met.

Ellery glanced up at the clock. 9:07.

He strolled over to her. "Don't show them you're worried. There's nothing to worry about. We have twenty-eight minutes." He raised his voice, smiling. "Naturally the thief has ditched the money, hoping to recover it when the coast is clear. It's therefore hidden somewhere in the classroom. All right, Miss Carpenter, we'll take the desks and seats first. Look under them too—chewing gum makes a handy adhesive. Eh, class?"

Four minutes later they looked at each other, then up at the clock.

9:11.

Exactly twenty-four minutes remaining.

"Well," said Ellery.

He began to ransack the room. Books, radiators, closets, supplies, lunchbags, schoolbags. Bulletin boards, wall maps, the terrestrial globe. The UN poster, the steel engravings of Washington and Lincoln. He even emptied Louise's three pots of geraniums and sifted the earth.

His eyes kept returning to the clock more and more often.

Ellery searched everything in the room, from the socket of the American flag to the insect-filled bowls of the old light fixtures, reached by standing on desks.

Everything.

"It's not here!" whispered Louise in his ear.

The Buell, Ruffo, and Strager boys were nudging one another, grinning.

"Well, well," Ellery said.

Interesting. Something of a problem at that.

Of course! He got up and checked two things he had

missed—the cup of the pencil sharpener and the grid covering the loudspeaker of the PA system. No envelope. No money.

He took out a handkerchief and wiped his neck.

Really it's a little silly. A schoolboy!

Ellery glanced at the clock.

9:29.

Six minutes left in which not only to find the money but identify the thief!

He leaned against Louise's desk, forcing himself to relax.

It was these "simple" problems. Nothing big and important, like murder, blackmail, bank robbery. A miserable seven dollars lifted by a teen-age delinquent in an overcrowded classroom . . .

He thought furiously.

Let the bell ring at 9:35 and the boy strut out of Miss Carpenter's room undetected, with his loot, and he would send up a howl like a wolf cub over his first kill. *Who says these big-shot law jerks ain't monkeys? The biggest! He's a lot of nothin'. Wind. See me stand him on his ear? And this is just for openers. Wait till I get goin' for real, not any of this kid stuff* . . .

No, nothing big and important like murder. Just seven dollars, and a big shot to laugh at. Not important? Ellery nibbled his lip. It was probably the most important case of his career.

9:30:30.

Only four and a half minutes left!

Louise Carpenter was gripping a desk, her knuckles white. Waiting to be let down.

Ellery pushed away from the desk and reached into the patch pocket of his tweed jacket for his pipe and tobacco, thinking harder about Helen McDoud's seven-dollar gift fund than he had ever thought about anything in his life.

And as he thought . . .

At 9:32 he was intently examining the rectangles of paper the thief had put into the substitute envelope. The paper was ordinary cheap newsprint, scissored to dollar-bill size out of a colored comics section. He shuffled through the dummy dollars one by one, hunting for something. Anything!

The forty-one boys and girls were buzzing and giggling now.

Ellery pounced. Clinging to one of the rectangles was a needle-thin sliver of paper about an inch long, a sort of paper shaving. He fingered it, held it up to the light. It was not newsprint. Too full-bodied, too tough-textured . . .

Then he knew what it must be.

Less than two minutes left.

Feverishly he went through the remaining dollar-sized strips of comic paper.

And there it was. There it was!

This strip had been cut from the top of the comic sheet. On the margin appeared the name of a New York newspaper and the date *April 24, 1955.*

Think it over. Take your time. Lots of seconds in a minute.

The buzzing and giggling had died. Louise Carpenter was on her feet, looking at him imploringly.

A bell began clanging in the corridor.

First period over.

9:35.

Ellery rose and said solemnly, "The case is solved."

With the room cleared and the door locked, the three boys stood backed against the blackboard as if facing a firing squad. The bloom was gone from David Strager's cheeks. The blood vessel in Joey Buell's temple was trying to wriggle into his red hair. And Howard Ruffo's eyes were liquid with panic.

It's hard to be fifteen years old and trapped.

But harder not to be.

"Wha'd I do?" whimpered Howard Ruffo. "I didn't do nothin'."

"We didn't take Miss Carpenter's seven dollars," said David Strager, stiff-lipped.

"Can you say the same about Mr. Mueller's baked goods last Monday night, Dave?" Ellery paused gently. "Or any of the other things you boys have been making love to in the past two months?"

He thought they were going to faint.

"But this morning's little job," Ellery turned suddenly to the red-haired boy, "you pulled by yourself, Joey."

The thin body quivered. "Who, me?"

"Yes, Joey, you."

"You got rocks in your skull," Joey whispered. "Not me!"

"I'll prove it, Joey. Hand me the dollar bill I found in your jeans when I searched you."

"That's my dollar!"

"I know it, Joey. I'll give you another for it. Hand it over . . . Miss Carpenter."

"Yes, Mr. Queen!"

"To cut these strips of newspaper to the same size as dollar bills, the thief must have used a real bill as a pattern. If he cut too close, the scissors would shave off a sliver of the bill." Ellery handed her Joey's dollar. "See if this bill shows a slight indentation along one edge."

"It does!"

"And I found this sliver clinging to one of the dummies. Fit the sliver to the indented edge of Joey's bill. If Joey is guilty, it should fit exactly. Does it?"

Louise looked at the boy. "Joey, it does fit."

David and Howard were gaping at Ellery.

"What a break," Joey choked.

"Criminals make their own bad breaks, Joey. The thing inside you that told you you were doing wrong made your hand shake as you cut. But even if your hand hadn't slipped, I'd have known you were the one who substituted the strips of paper for the money."

"How? How could you?" It was a cry of bewilderment.

Ellery showed him the rectangular strip with the white margin. "See this, Joey? Here's the name of the newspaper, and the date is *April 24, 1955*. What date is today?"

"Friday the 22nd . . ."

"Friday, April 22nd. But these strips of colored comics come from the newspaper of April 24th, Joey—*this coming Sunday's paper*. Who gets advance copies of the Sunday comics? Stores that sell newspapers in quantity. Getting the bulldog editions in advance gives them a jump on the Sunday morning rush, when they have to insert the news sections.

"Nothing to it, Joey. Which of you three boys had access before this morning to next Sunday's bulldog editions? Not David—he works in a supermarket. Not Howard—he works for a dry cleaner. But you work in a big cigar and stationery store, Joey, where newspapers must be one of the stock items."

Joey Buell's eyes glassed over.

"We think we're strong, Joey, and then we run into somebody stronger," Ellery said. "We think we're the smartest, and someone comes along to outsmart us. We beat the rap a dozen times, but the thirteenth time the rap beats us. You can't win, Joey."

Joey burst into tears.

Louise Carpenter made an instinctive gesture toward him. Ellery's head-shake warned her back. He went close to the boy and tousled the red head, murmuring something the others could not hear. And after a while Joey's tears sniffled to an end and he wiped his eyes on his sleeve in a puzzled way.

"Because I think this is going to work out all right, Joey,"

Ellery said, continuing their curious colloquy aloud. "We'll have a session with Mr. Hinsdale, and then with some pretty right guys I happen to know at Police Headquarters. After that it will be up to you."

Joey Buell gulped. "Okay, Mr. Queen." He did not look at his two friends.

David and Howard communicated silently. Then David turned to Ellery. "Where do we stand, Mr. Queen?"

"You and Howard are coming along."

The blond boy bit his lip. Then he nodded, and after a moment the dark boy nodded, too.

"Oh, I almost forgot." Ellery dipped briskly into the jacket pocket that held his pipe and tobacco. His hand reappeared with a wrinkled envelope, its flap written over. From the envelope protruded the corners of some one-dollar bills. "Your Helen McDoud wedding gift fund, Miss Carpenter. With Joey's compliments."

"I did forget!" gasped Louise. "Where did you find it?"

"Where Joey in desperation slipped it as I was frisking the other boys. The only thing in the room I didn't think of searching—my own pocket." Ellery winked at the three boys. "Coming, fellas?"

No Parking

Modesta Ryan played her greatest role not on a Broadway stage but in her penthouse off Madison Avenue. The performance took place one midsummer night against a backdrop of flooding rain, thunder, and lightning; power failures darkened some buildings in the Central Park area; and, of course, the Athenia Apartments was one of them. So Modesta even got to play her big scene by the light of candles, a surefire touch.

Ellery was not surprised. Modesta Ryan specialized in melodrama. Everything she touched went off like a rocket. She could not walk her dog without landing on the front page. Her last pet had broken his leash on Fifth Avenue and been run over by a car carrying the ambassador of an Iron Curtain country.

Modesta was spectacularly unlucky in love. She had never married. The men she wanted always seemed to prefer lisping ingénues or hat-check girls, and those who wanted her she could not stand. Her suitors ran to hand-kissers, cigaret-hold-er smokers, jodhpur-wearers, and gloomy college boys with mother fixations.

But suddenly, there he was. It was too impossibly wonderful. There he was—all three of him.

For naturally, when the right man did come along, two others equally right showed up, too.

It was a typical Modesta Ryan sensation, and for some months Broadway speculated on little else. Which of the three would she marry?

Jock Shanville was male lead in the new play Modesta was rehearsing, a costume piece set in medieval Venice. It was type-casting, for besides flaunting a doge's profile, a wicked eye, and a fine leg in tights, Shanville excelled in scene-stealing, reputation-poisoning, character assassination, and other closet arts of the theater. Jock had a wife, an ex-show girl named Pearline, but she was no problem; his rapier tongue had been backing her toward the nearest divorce court long before he decided on Modesta Ryan as her successor.

Then there was Kid Catt, a black-browed fighting machine who dealt bloody unconsciousness from both fists with a cold smile that had become his TV trademark. The Kid's body was his god, self-denial his creed; and women sat high on his proscribed list. So when he fell in love with Modesta it was with the violent passion of a fallen monk. Modesta found holding the beautiful young brute at bay an enchanting experience.

Richard Van Olde II, however, was a quite different temptation. Van Olde was a soft-spoken tyrant of position and wealth. Modesta Ryan was the first woman he had wanted since the death of his wife a dozen years before, and he meant to have her. He was a man of instant, irrevocable decisions, and he offered Modesta marriage from the first, courting her tirelessly. There was something about his lashless eyes and noiseless personality that made her shiver like an inexperienced girl.

Jock Shanville fitted her like a glove, young Catt excited her, Van Olde fascinated her.

Which should she accept?

The phone rang just as Ellery was stooping to unlace his shoes.

"It's for you," Inspector Queen called from the other bedroom.

"At a quarter to twelve?" Ellery used the extension. "Yes?"

"Ellery? Modesta Ryan . . ."

"Modesta." Ellery fingered his tie automatically. He had

known her for years, and each time he heard her voice was like the first time. Tonight the throaty tones had a throb in them, subdued and off-beat. "What's wrong?"

"Ellery, I'm in trouble," she whispered. "Can you come right over to my apartment? Please."

"Of course. But what kind of trouble?"

"I can't talk. I'm not alone—"

"This marriage business?"

"Yes, I decided today. Gave the other two their walking papers. But hurry!"

"Modesta, wait. Just tell me who's with you—"

But the phone went dead. Ellery grabbed his raincoat and ran.

The streets were empty rivers, and he roared east toward Central Park leaving a wake like a power launch. He was through the park transverse and across Fifth and Madison Avenues in a matter of minutes. Sixty seconds later he was sloshing around the corner of Park Avenue into a one-way westbound street in the East Eighties, peering through his streaming windshield for a parking space.

As far down the street as he could see, the curbs were jammed with cars bumper to bumper.

Ellery cruised, trying to control his temper. You could never find a parking space in New York, least of all when you were in a hurry. And when it rained—

The Athenia Apartments was on the northeast corner, just off Madison Avenue. Between the corner and the Athenia's canopy he sighted empty curb and he stepped on the gas. But when he got there he saw a No Parking sign; it was a crosstown bus stop. Wouldn't you know! Back into Madison Avenue he drove, and he circumnavigated the block, ready to settle for a dozen feet of curb anywhere. But the curbs were all occupied. He turned into Modesta's street again, worried and furious.

God knows what's happening up there, he thought angrily. He was tempted to park at the bus stop; but a family respect for the law, and the prospect of squatting half a day in Traffic Court, dissuaded him.

No miracle had happened. There was still no place to park on Modesta's street. Groaning, Ellery turned up Madison Avenue again.

"This is my last time on this merry-go-round," he promised himself grittily. "Modesta must think I'm coming by pack mule. I'll double-park."

The last time around he had noticed one car illegally parked. At the curb between the Athenia's canopy and the entrance of the next building stood three cars in a row, and a fourth was double-parked by the side of the middle one. The double-parked car bore an M.D. license plate.

Again Ellery drove up the block from Park Avenue toward Madison. He was about to pull in behind the doctor's car when two young couples dashed out of the apartment house on the southeast corner, splashed toward the Athenia's canopy, and jumped into the first of the three parked cars.

"Hurray," Ellery said sourly; and when his rescuers pulled away he shot around the double-parked car and backed like a fireman into the vacated space nearest the canopy.

Five minutes past midnight! He had lost ten minutes finding a space. And he'd been lucky at that.

Ellery was under the Athenia's canopy in two jumps. He ran into the lobby, swishing the water off his hat. The lobby was dark. Basement flooded, probably, shorting the power mains.

"Doorman?" he shouted into the darkness.

"Comin'." A flashlight snapped on and bobbed quickly toward him. "Who'd you want to see, sir?"

"Miss Ryan, penthouse. Elevator out?"

"Uh-huh." The doorman seemed dubious. "It's pretty late. The house phone's not working, either."

"I'm expected," said Ellery. "Where's the stairway? Speak up!"

The doorman stared, then mumbled, "This way."

The man shuffled toward the rear of the lobby, past the dead switchboard, directing his light behind him for Ellery. As they reached the emergency door it opened and a male figure hurried past them and vanished in the darkness. Ellery caught one glimpse of the figure as it scuttled by—stooped over, so that his height and age were impossible to guess, wearing a double-breasted tan trench coat buttoned up the left side to the chin, and a tan Stetson pulled well down over his face.

Something about the man bothered Ellery, but he had no time to analyze.

He ran up marble stairs endlessly, praying that the battery of his pencil-flashlight would hold out. When he reached the penthouse landing eleven flights up he was seeing phosphorescent confetti in the darkness. Breathing hard, he swept his light about, located the pushbutton near the service door, and leaned on it. He heard a buzz inside the apartment, but nothing else.

He tried the door. It was unlocked.

Ellery stepped into Modesta Ryan's country-style kitchen.

A candle-glass was wavering eerily on the fireplace mantel; a bed of briquets had burned to embers.

"Modesta?"

He stepped through the swinging door into her dining room, feeling his scalp tickle. A candlestick on the sideboard illuminated the room fitfully. The hall beyond was dark.

"Modesta?"

He groped along the passage, playing his flash, no longer calling. He kept telling himself as the shadows parted in his path that Modesta was quite capable of an elaborate joke, picking a night like this for atmosphere.

For a moment, as he stepped into her living room, he was sure of it. Two seven-branched candelabra blazed, and in the focus of their flames, in an exquisite negligee, lay Modesta's lovely body. She was crumpled on the Italian-tile floor beside her mother-of-pearl grand piano. On the breast of her negligee there was an illusion of a bullet wound and blood . . . Ellery knelt. The stuff staining her breast looked exactly like ketchup.

But it was not. And the silk was scorched around a very real hole.

He hunted for her pulse. There it was!—but it was flickering like the candles. She was barely alive.

Ellery ran to the phone more out of habit than conviction. To his surprise it was working. He made two calls—one for an emergency ambulance, the other to his father; and then he tore through the apartment to the service door and began leaping down the eleven flights like a mountain goat.

If she dies, he was thinking, those parked cars around here ought to be tagged as accessories. The ten minutes he had lost looking for a parking space might have saved what was left of Modesta Ryan's life.

He plunged out under the canopy, followed by the astonished doorman. Nothing had changed. The cloudburst continued to swab down the streets. The same three cars were lined up between the Athenia's entrance and the adjoining building, his own foremost; the same doctor's car was still double-parked beside the middle car of the three, boxing it in.

Of course the man in the trench coat was gone.

"Then this is the way it went, Wladeczki?" Inspector Queen said to the doorman in the light of the police torches. "You were on duty since four P.M., due to go off at midnight, but you stayed on because the storm held up your relief man. You didn't leave this lobby at any time. Nobody could have sneaked past you. All right.

"Miss Ryan came home from rehearsal in a taxi about seven P.M. She was alone. About eight her maid left for the night. Between eight and a few minutes past eleven only five people entered or left the building. They are all long-time tenants. At eleven-thirty Mr. Trench Coat walks into the lobby. Five minutes later an M.D. on emergency call to an old lady tenant—who's very sick in 4-G—drives up and complains to you he can't find space for his car. You let the doctor double-park—"

"And he's still up in 4-G," said Sergeant Velie. "The other five, the tenants, alibi okay, too."

"Now about Mr. Trench Coat. He didn't come by cab, you say. You don't get a real good look at him by your flash, the way he has his hat pulled down and his collar turned up. He talks in a croaky whisper, as if he has a bad cold. He says he has an appointment with Miss Modesta Ryan, you tell him he'll have to walk up to the penthouse, he goes up the stairway, and that's the last you see of him till a few minutes past midnight when he ducks out the stairway door under your nose—and the nose," added the Inspector gently, "of the eminent Mr. Queen here."

Ellery gave his father a wan look. "Did you notice," he asked the doorman, "how wet his trench coat and hat were when he first came into the lobby?"

"No wetter than yours was, Mr. Queen," said the doorman. "Got my name spelled right, Sergeant?"

"Time will tell," said the Sergeant. "Hey, Goldie. Well?"

Detective Goldberg came in, shaking himself like a dog. He had found Modesta Ryan's maid asleep in her Harlem flat, he reported; the maid knew nothing except that on Miss Ryan's arrival home she had made three phone calls—one to Kid Catt, one to Mr. Shanville, and the last to Mr. Van Olde. But the maid hadn't listened to the conversations, so she couldn't say which ones Miss Ryan had given the heave and which one she'd made the happy man.

"Any report from the hospital yet?" muttered the Inspector.

"She's this way that way," said Sergeant Velie.

"But did she talk?"

"She's got all she can do to keep on breathing, Inspector. She's still unconscious."

"Then we do it the hard way," said the old man gloomily. "It's a cinch Trench Coat was one of Modesta's two rejects. He didn't waste any time, did he? As soon as those three are brought in, have 'em taken up to the penthouse. Coming, Ellery?"

His son sighed. "If I could have found a place to park as soon as I got here . . ."

Hollow laughter followed him to the stairway door.

At twenty minutes after two the Inspector finished with the last of the three interrogations. He found Ellery in Modesta Ryan's living room staring reproachfully at her phone.

"Any luck?"

"I've called every columnist in town, all her close friends. She just didn't tell anybody."

The old man grunted. He stuck his head into the hall. "Get those cuties in here."

Shanville made his entrance with a rather set smile. The disheveled blond hair was all dagger points, and with the slight upcurve of his lips he looked Satanic.

"What now?" he asked. "The rack?"

About Kid Catt there was a look of astounded suffering, as if he had just been knocked down. His powerful frame sagged into a chair and his black eyes stared dully at the chalkmarks on the tiles near the piano.

"Who did it?" the fighter mumbled. "Just tell me which one of these two did it."

"Underplay, Kid," said the actor pleasantly. "This is a professional audience."

The black eyes looked at him. "Lay off, actor," the Kid said.

"Or else?" smiled Shanville.

"I'm leaving," said Richard Van Olde II abruptly.

The tycoon was very angry. His naturally pale skin was almost green, the lashless eyes murderous.

"Just another few minutes, Mr. Van Olde," said Inspector Queen.

"A very few, please. Then I either walk out of here unmolested or I telephone my attorneys and the Commissioner."

"Yes, *sir*. Now, gentlemen, each of you wanted to marry Miss Ryan—bad. And each of you got a phone call from her tonight. One she told she'd finally decided to marry. Two— the other two—she brushed. One of those two promptly came here tonight and shot her.

"You think you've got us stymied," the Inspector went on, showing his dentures. "Each man was found home in bed. And while we have the bullet—probably from a .38—search of your respective premises has failed to turn up the gun. Or the trench coat or Stetson. On top of that, each claims *he* was the man Modesta told over the phone she was accepting! Two of those claims are lies, of course, to take the heat off.

"Gentlemen, I have news for you," said Inspector Queen softly. "Thrown-away guns, coats, and hats have a way of turning up. And you've got no alibis for the time of the shooting. You were home in bed, say all of you, but none of you can prove it, not even you, Shanville, because you occupy a separate bedroom and weren't even heard coming home——"

"Dad."

The Inspector looked around, surprised. Ellery was on his feet, the picture of wry hopelessness.

"I don't see any point to going any further with this now, do you? Let's call it a night. These gentlemen won't run away, and we can all use some sleep."

The old man blinked.

"All right," he said.

But when the three had gone, he growled to his son, "And what's the big plot, Master Mind?"

"It's simple enough," Ellery said as they crouched near the glass outer doors of the lobby. It was after three, the rain had stopped, and the chrome on the dark cars outside winked damply in the street lights. "We're waiting for our friend to come back."

"Come *back?*" said Sergeant Velie. "What is he, goofed?"

"Case of necessity, Velie," murmured Ellery. "Consider. How did Trench Coat get to the Athenia——?"

"*Get* here?"

"Yes. By cab? No, says the doorman. On foot? No, because if he'd walked or even run from as close by as the corner of Madison he'd have been soaked in that downpour, whereas the doorman said his trench coat and hat were no wetter than mine when I got here——and I had to make only two jumps from my car to get under the canopy. Conclusion? *Trench Coat came in a car, and he parked almost as close to the canopy as I did.*"

His father made a strangled sound.

"Now, the nearest parked cars are those four between the Athenia's canopy and the next building——my car, the two behind mine, and the M.D.'s, double-parked beside the one behind mine. Well, which of the four was Trench Coat's? Not mine, of course, or the car mine replaced——the people who drove off in that one came from the building across the street; what's more, they drove away before Trench Coat left the Athenia.

"So Trench Coat's car must be one of the other three. Which one?

"Let's see. Trench Coat made his escape just as I was going up to Modesta's apartment. You'd expect him to jump into his car—one of those three—and drive off. Did he? No —when I rushed downstairs after finding Modesta shot, all three cars were still parked. Why didn't he take his car for his getaway? *Obviously, because he couldn't.* His car must be the one behind mine, the middle one of the three at the curb —the one that's boxed in by the doctor's car!"

The Inspector sounded punchy. "So that's why you moved your jalopy away . . . to give him room to get his car out when he thinks the coast is clear."

"That's the idea," said Ellery.

"Now all you have to do," said the Sergeant, not without bitterness, "is tell us who you see in your crystal ball."

"Why, So-and-So," replied Ellery, naming a name; and at their exclamations he grinned. "At least, I'm ninety-nine percent sure."

At four-fifteen A.M. a furtive figure skulked suddenly past the Athenia, darted into the designated car, and fought cattishly but in vain to shake off Sergeant Velie's paralyzing clutch.

It was, as Ellery had predicted, So-and-So.

By the time they booked their catch downtown and sat in on the confession, the city was driving to work. They crawled uptown in Ellery's car to the hospital.

It was while Inspector Queen went off to inquire about Modesta that Sergeant Velie seemed to come out of a fog. "Can I be *that* stupid, Ellery? I still don't see how—"

"Console yourself," soothed Ellery. "The doorman and I saw Trench Coat; you didn't. When he hurried past us at the stairway door, I was bothered by something in his appearance. Later I realized what it had been: he'd had his double-breasted coat buttoned down the *left* side. It's women who are left-side buttoners; men are the reverse. So I knew Trench Coat was a woman dressed as a man. Which woman? Van Olde's a widower, Kid Catt's a bachelor, and neither has any entangling alliances. But Jock Shanville's married, so his wife was an odds-on bet. As she told us, she eavesdropped on Modesta's call, heard that she was through as Mrs. Shanville, and proceeded—with the help of her theatrical training—to do something about it."

The Sergeant was still shaking his head when the Inspector came back, all smiles. Modesta would live—although she'd have to have new evening gowns designed—and she had satisfactorily fingered Pearline Shanville as the jealous witch who had ruined her décolletage.

Then they shuffled blearily out to Ellery's car and he found a ticket on it for parking in a restricted hospital zone.

No Place to Live

When they entered the flat they were after someone else altogether. But in one of the rooms off the center hall they found a man with half his head blown off, and over him a pretty blonde with a cheap new wedding band on her left hand holding the cannon.

Sergeant Velie took the gun from her by the barrel delicately, and Inspector Queen looked at her ring and said to her, "And you're Mrs.—?"

"Graham," the girl said. "June Graham."

Ellery caught June Graham as she fell.

Twenty-four hours earlier Brock was on his unmade bed doping the next day's fourth race when his landlord came to call.

Brock went out and opened the apartment door. He had a broken nose and he was dressed in pink and brown.

"If it ain't Mr. Finger," Brock said, surprised. "You come to investigate my cockroaches personally?"

Mr. Finger stepped into Brock's flat in ominous silence. Brock hustled him into the dirty bedroom and shut the door.

"What's on your mind?" Brock said.

"Rent." Mr. Finger was small and fat and wore a big ruby on his right hand. He owned eight apartment houses on the upper West Side. *Their* rent, Mr. Brock."

Brock followed the line of his landlord's fat thumb and it told him the whole sad story. "So Jerky talked," Brock said.

"If you're meaning my super, yeah," Mr. Finger said in a chilling voice. "Look, Brock, you been behind my back renting out three of your five rooms. This is against the law."

"You don't mean it," Brock said.

Mr. Finger began ticking off invisible subtenants. "Mrs. Wodjeska, no husband, two kids, cleans offices at night— some subtenant! A no-good that calls himself Smith. Smith, ha! A G.I. and his wife name of Graham, just back from the service. Brock, those six didn't sign no lease with Harvey Finger."

"Let's talk this over," Brock said, showing his gold-capped teeth.

"So we're talking, ain't we?" the landlord said. "Twenty-five dollars a week per room you're charging. That's a monthly income to you of around three twenty-five. My super you smear forty a month. Me you pay the frozen rent of eighty-five. I didn't even graduate public school, Mr. Brock, but even I can figure your net profit on my apartment is two hundred bucks a month. So tell me one reason why I shouldn't report you to the State Temporary Rent Commission?"

"Aw, get smart," Brock said. "So I'm dispossessed. So they let you sign on a new tenant at a great big twelve dollars and seventy-five cents more a month, and you'll maybe have to redecorate, fix the plumbing, check the wiring, and God knows. Mr. Finger, what's the percentage?"

Mr. Finger said softly, "Fifty-fifty."

Brock got him, all right. "Robber!"

"Can names hurt me?" The landlord shrugged. "It's one hundred a month extra from you, or you're out on your ear."

"Fifty. Not a nickel more!"

"Hundred."

"Seventy-five——"

"I'm a one-price landlord," Mr. Finger said, not without humor. "Is it pay, Mr. Brock, or on your way, Mr. Brock?"

Brock kicked the armchair. It was his own chair, so Mr. Finger waited unperturbed.

"The goats ain't been running for me," Brock growled. "I got to have time to scrape it up."

"Scrape fast," Mr. Finger said, smiling. He turned at the door. "You got till eight o'clock tomorrow night."

"Big deal," Brock said bitterly.

He waited till the fat little man was gone and then he stalked up the hall and shoved Mrs. Wodjeska's door open. Mrs. Wodjeska was in bed being fed some soup by a little girl while another little girl applied cold compresses to her mother's head. When the two little girls saw who it was they stopped what they were doing and ran to hide behind the lopsided sofa.

"Can't you ever knock?" the woman said hoarsely.

Brock scowled. "You still sick?"

"It's the virus." Mrs. Wodjeska pulled the covers up to her chin. "What do you want?"

"My rent."

"I'll pay you next week."

"Listen, you, I been kidded by experts. What's the score?"

"Tomorrow I'm promised a job. Will you please go? You're scaring my children."

"Now I scare kids!" Brock said in an injured tone. "Look, Mrs. Social Register, I need this rent, see? You pay up by tomorrow night or bed your kids down on the sidewalk. This ain't the Salvation Army!"

Brock was figuring other angles when Hank Graham, the lanky ex-G.I., burst in on him.

"Okay, Brock," Graham said, glaring. "Where is it?"

Graham was twenty pounds lighter than Brock, but something in the thrust of his jaw made Brock step behind the armchair.

"Where is what?" Brock asked cautiously.

"My money!" Hank Graham said. "And don't play dumb with me, buddy. I want the three thousand dollars you swiped from my room, and I want it now."

"Hold it, hold it," Brock murmured. "You got three grand?"

"Savings. I brought it back from Germany last month and got married on the strength of it. Nobody knew about that money, Brock, not even my wife. I was keeping it for a down payment on a house in Jersey as a surprise to Juney. All of a sudden it's gone from where I hid it in my room, and you're the only one with a duplicate key to the lock!"

"First I hear of it," Brock said absently.

Young Graham advanced on the chair. "Give, you crook, or I call the police."

"Keep your shirt on, General. I didn't take your three grand. But I got a pretty good idea who did."

"And who would that be?"

"My experience is you check first and make with the names later," Brock said. "Look, Graham, yell copper and you may never see a cent. But give me time and I think I can get it back for you."

Hank Graham looked him over.

"Tomorrow night," he said grimly. "Then it's either my money back or you'll explain in a police station."

Through a crack in his door Brock watched the ex-G.I. trudge back to his room. Pretty June Graham was waiting in their doorway. She was in a clinging negligee and Brock automatically inventoried her curves. He saw her ask her husband something in a puzzled way, and Graham's forced smile; then they went into their room and locked the door.

Brock waited.

He stole up the hall and scratched on the last door.

"Open up, Smith," he said in a soft voice. "It's Brock."

He grinned when he heard the chain rattle. Installing a chain latch had been Smith's own idea.

Smith glanced swiftly down the hall before he motioned Brock into his room and relatched the door. Smith was a dark skinny man with holes for eyes.

"What do *you* want?" He had a nasty voice.

"Graham's three grand."

"What, what?" Smith said excitedly.

Brock reached down to fix Smith's egg-stained tie. "I know I didn't take it, and it wasn't the Wodjeska number—what crook scrubs floors for a living? So that leaves you, Smitty. No three-buck lock would keep *you* out of the Grahams' room."

"You're on the junk," Smith jeered, trying to back off. "I don't know nothing about no three grand—"

Brock pulled Smith's tie tight, using both hands. Smith's eyes bugged and he began to turn blue, legs jerking.

"You little punk," Brock smiled, "how long do you think it took me to spot you?—a guy who don't stick his nose out from one day to another except for a couple minutes at night sometimes. You're Ratsy Johnson, Frank Pompo's fingerman. Inspector Queen's been looking for you since early summer to testify in the case he got up against Pompo for the D.A., and so's Pompo to see that you don't. Do you shell out Graham's three grand or do I tip off Queen *and* Pompo where you're hiding out?"

Johnson pointed frantically to his throat. Brock loosened his hold a little.

"I'll make a deal," the fugitive gasped.

"With what?"

"With a frame, that's with what! Brock, without moola I'll chance the D.A. I'm down to shoe buttons. You hog this bundle and I'll surrender to the law and say you fixed it for me to hide out in your place! See?"

Brock thought. Then he let go.

"Okay, I'll chisel the kid into settling for one grand of his dough, and I'll give you five C's for your end."

Ratsy Johnson fingered his neck. "We split even up, see?"

"You're a hard man," Brock mourned. "Where's the take?"

Johnson produced a cheap cigaret case. From it he extracted a stained king-size cigaret and peeled the paper down. The gap revealed a tuft of tobacco on one end, a filter at the other, and a green paper tube between. He unrolled the tube and it became three one-thousand-dollar bills. Brock snatched them, then looked down at his fingers. The oily stain on the cigaret paper was also on the outer bill.

"What do you smoke, fuel oil?" Brock wrapped the bills in a silk handkerchief and tucked it all carefully away.

Johnson clawed at him. "Give me mine, you chiseler!"

Brock's big hand chopped down and Johnson fell like a clubbed fish. "What's the uproar, Ratsy? You get yours when I con Graham into the deal. Maybe he won't play."

"Okay, okay," the fugitive sniveled from the floor. "But you double-cross me, Brock, and so help me——"

Brock went out grinning.

That was a Tuesday night.

On Wednesday one of Sergeant Velie's regular stoolies had passed the word that Ratsy Johnson was holed up in Apartment 4-A of a tenement on the West Side. Velie had had the house staked out since Wednesday afternoon, waiting for Johnson to show. He was not known to be armed but he was considered dangerous and the street seemed a safer place to take him. Detectives were planted on the roof, the fourth floor, and in the lobby. Because of the importance of the arrest Inspector Queen showed up to take personal charge, and Ellery tagged along.

At 8:30 p.m. the Inspector decided not to wait any longer and they had entered Apartment 4-A to find not only Ratsy Johnson but the body of Charlie the Chiseler Brock. Brock had been shot with a .45 automatic at close quarters through one of his pillows, used by his killer to muffle the report. His body was still warm.

In the first few minutes they learned all about Brock's illegal subrentals of three of his five rooms and the events of the night before. Brock's threat to put Mrs. Wodjeska and her children on the street for nonpayment of rent came out in a rush. The theft of Hank Graham's three thousand dollars had been registered by the aggrieved ex-G.I. immediately. Even landlord Finger's ultimatum to Brock twenty-four hours earlier was in Sergeant Velie's notebook, Mr. Finger deciding that candor about a little rent conspiracy was preferable to being mixed up in a murder.

And Ratsy Johnson, found cowering in his room, meekly undid the chain with his own hands and apparently was so overwhelmed by his plight—caught by the police, hunted by boss mobster Frank Pompo, and now up to his stringy neck in a murder rap—that he confessed his theft of young Graham's money and told all about his Tuesday night deal with Brock.

It was all very clear—except who was lying about what

went on in Charlie the Chiseler Brock's dirty bedroom between 8:00 and 8:30 Wednesday evening.

Landlord Harvey Finger had arrived at the apartment house for his payoff from Brock a few minutes before 8:00 P.M. He had been permitted to enter 4-A, but on coming out a few minutes later he was stopped by detectives; and after Brock's corpse was found at 8:30, when they entered the apartment to arrest Johnson, the little fat landlord insisted he had left Brock alive.

Hank Graham said he had visited Brock's room after Finger's departure, spoken to Brock for five minutes or so, and claimed he too had left Brock alive.

Ratsy Johnson said he had not seen Brock on Wednesday evening at all, and Mrs. Wodjeska said the same thing. The hoodlum had no alibi, and Mrs. Wodjeska's two little girls could not corroborate their mother's claim, as they had been playing hopscotch all evening in the alley behind the tenement with other children.

So it all came back to the pretty blond girl found standing over the body, the gun in her hand.

She had been revived by Ellery and her frantic husband and now she was in one of Brock's chairs, pale and trembling.

"Why did you kill this man?" Inspector Queen said to her.

"She didn't kill him," Hank Graham shouted, "and for God's sake cover him up."

Sergeant Velie obliged with the evening paper.

"I didn't kill him," Juney Graham said, not looking. "I came in here to talk to him and this is what I found."

"And the gun?" Ellery asked gently.

"It was on the floor and I picked it up."

"Why?"

She did not reply.

"Innocent people who walk in on corpses and immediately pick up the gun are common in the movies and television," Ellery said, "but in real life they'd rather pick up a live rattlesnake. Why did you pick up the gun, Mrs. Graham?"

The girl's hands twisted. "I—I don't know. I wasn't thinking, I guess."

"Did you ever see the gun before?" Inspector Queen asked. "No."

It went on that way for some time.

"Now as I get it," Inspector Queen said to Hank Graham's pretty bride, "your husband went to Brock's room to demand the return of his three thousand dollars that Brock had promised to get back. Brock offered him a thousand dollars in settlement, your husband lost his temper and refused, and he came rushing back to your room all set to call the police. And that was when he told you he'd saved three thousand dollars of his overseas pay and it had been stolen from him, Mrs. Graham? That's the first you knew about the whole thing?"

June Graham nodded stiffly.

"Why did you talk your husband out of calling the police?"

"I was afraid Hank would get beaten up or—or something. I never did want to rent this room. I didn't like Brock's looks."

Sergeant Velie had been studying the girl's curves. "Brock ever make a pass at you?"

"No! I mean—well, once, when Hank was out. I slapped his face and he walked out laughing. But he never tried it again."

"You didn't tell me that," Hank Graham said slowly.

Inspector Queen and his son exchanged glances.

"Now about that gun, Mrs. Graham," Ellery began.

"I've told you about the gun!"

"You talked your husband out of phoning the police and you went to Brock's room to see what you could do," the Inspector said. "Take it from there."

"But I've told you!"

"Tell us again."

"I knocked," June Graham said wearily. "He didn't answer. I tried the door. It opened. I went in. He was lying on the floor all . . . all messy. There was a gun beside the body. I picked it up and then you all came in."

"Why did you pick up the gun, Mrs. Graham?"

"I don't *know*, I tell you."

"Then suppose I tell you," Ellery said. "You picked it up because you recognized it."

"No!" It was almost a scream.

"Instead of bulldozing the poor kid," Hank Graham muttered, "why don't you find my three thousand dollars?"

"Oh, we found them, Graham. We found them right here in Brock's room, stashed under the arch support of an alligator shoe. The shoe, by the way, was on Brock's foot." Inspector Queen smiled. "But let's not change the subject, Graham. Your wife is lying about that gun."

"I'm not!" the girl said despairingly. "I never saw it before."

"Good try, Mrs. Graham," Ellery said, "but not good

enough. The fact is it's your husband's gun—an Army .45. When you found it beside Brock's body after Hank had been arguing with him, you naturally thought Hank had shot him. Isn't that it?"

"Hank, no! Don't!"

"No use, honey." Hank Graham shook his head. "Okay, Mr. Queen, it's my gun. But I didn't shoot Brock. I left him alive."

"That's your story," Inspector Queen said sadly, for he was a notorious softie about young love. But he signaled Sergeant Velie.

"Hank!" The girl flew to him and clung, sobbing.

"A story with one chapter missing," Ellery said, eying June Graham tenderly. "You left something out, Graham."

Hank Graham was stroking his wife's hair. He did not bother to look up. "Did I?"

"Yes. The one fact that clears you, you idiot, and pins this murder where it belongs!"

And Ellery had them bring Brock's killer in.

"You kept saying your money was stolen from where you'd hidden it in your room, Graham, and Johnson admitted he'd been the thief. But what you forgot to tell us, and what Johnson carefully neglected to say, was where in your room the money was hidden."

He requisitioned the official envelope containing the evidence and from it he took Graham's money.

"These three one-thousand-dollar bills were tightly rolled up, and the top bill is oil-stained," Ellery said. "You'd therefore hidden your money, Graham, in something narrow and tubelike whose insides are oily. Hank, why didn't you tell us you'd rolled up the bills *and slipped them into the barrel of your .45 for safekeeping?*"

"Holy smokes," Hank groaned.

"Then it wasn't money Ratsy Johnson was after when he went on the prowl in your room, it was your .45. He had no gun and he figured a newly returned G.I. might have one. It was only when he examined the .45 later that he found the three bills in the barrel.

"So the money places the gun that shot Brock in your possession, Ratsy," Ellery said to the suddenly green-faced fugitive. "You sneaked into Brock's room after Graham left tonight, shot Brock, looked for the money he'd hijacked from you, couldn't find it, lost your nerve, and ducked back to your room. Juney Graham must have just missed seeing you as she went to Brock's room to find him dead." Ellery turned and grinned at the newlyweds. "Any questions?"

"Yes," Hank Graham said, drying his wife's tears. "Anybody know where I can find an honest real estate agent?"

Miracles Do Happen

The moment Henry pecked her cheek that night, Claire knew something was wrong. But all she said was a wifely, "How did it go at the office today, dear?"

"All right," Henry Witter said, and Claire knew it was not the office. "What kind of day did Jody have?"

"About the same, dear."

Henry put his coat, hat, and rubbers in the hall closet while the other three children hunted through his pockets for the candy bars he always brought home on paydays.

"It's the teentsy size again," little Sal lisped indignantly.

"I wanna big one!" five-year-old Pete wailed.

Eddie, who was ten and knew the financial facts of life, merely scuttled off with his share of the loot.

"Aren't you two ashamed?" Claire said to Sal and Pete.

But Henry said in a queer voice, "Why should they be? It's true," and he went into the back bedroom to see Jody, who had been lying there for the last three of her eight years.

After dinner, which was beans baked around an irreducible minimum of Mr. Scholte's cheapest shortribs, Claire put Sal and Pete to bed, parked Eddie at the TV set, fixed Jody for the night, and hurried back to the kitchen. She helped Henry finish the dishes, and then the Witters sat down at the kitchen table for their weekly session—Claire with her budget notes, Henry with paper and pencil and his pay check between them.

Claire read off the items in a loud and casual voice, and Henry wrote them down in his bookkeeper's copperplate. The prorated expenses—rent, gas, electricity, telephone, TV installment, life insurance, health plan, personal loans. The running expenses—food, laundry, Henry's allowance. The "extras"—new shoes for Pete, school notebook for Eddie, repairs for the vacuum cleaner. And then—in that dread separate column headed "Jody"—medicines, therapist, installment on surgeon's fee for last operation . . .

Henry added the two columns in silence.

"Expenses, $89.61. Take-home pay, $82.25. Debit balance, $7.36." And Henry's tic began to act up.

Claire started to say something, but she swallowed it. It was the Jody column again. Without the Jody column they would be in the black, have a small savings account, and the children could get the clothes they desperately needed . . . Claire shut *those* thoughts off.

Henry cleared his throat. "Claire," he began.

"No," Claire cried. *"No,* Henry! Maybe you've given up hope on Jody, but I haven't. I'm *not* going to send a child of mine to a state institution, no matter what. She needs her family—the love and help we can give her—and maybe some day . . . Hen, we'll have the phone taken out, or send the TV back. You're due for another raise in a few months. We can hold out."

"Who said anything about sending Jody away?" Henry's voice was very queer indeed, and Claire felt a chill. "It's not that, Claire."

"Then what is it? I knew there was something wrong the minute you came home."

"It's Tully. He phoned me at the office this afternoon."

"Tully." Claire sat still. Last year, when Jody had needed her second operation and they had exhausted the annual health plan benefits, Henry had been forced to go to a loan shark for the money. "What's he want?"

"I don't know." Henry reached for his cigarets. But then he remembered that he had smoked his quota for the day, and he put the pack back in his pocket. "He just said for me to be at his office tomorrow night—at seven o'clock."

"But you paid him last month's interest on the loan. Or—did you, Henry?"

"Of course I did!"

"Then why—?"

"I don't know, I tell you!"

Dear God, Claire thought, nothing more *now*, please. She got up to go over to Henry and put her cracked and reddened hands on his thin shoulders.

"Darling . . . don't worry."

Henry said, "Who's worrying?" But he wished his tic would stop.

"Sit down, Witter." Tully indicated the only other chair in the dingy office. He had Henry's folder on his desk and was leafing through it.

Henry sat down. The room held nothing but an old desk and swivel chair, a filing cabinet, a big metal wastebasket, a costumer, and the "client's chair"—yet it always managed to seem crowded. Everything looked cheap, used hard, rubbed off, like Tully himself. The loan shark was a paper-thin man with eyes like rusty razor blades.

"Nice clean file," Tully said, tossing it aside.

"I try to meet my payments on time." Henry thought of all the empty-stomached lunch hours, the cigaret rations, Claire's incredible economies, the children's patched clothes, and he felt a gust of anger. "Just what is it you want, Mr. Tully?"

"The principal," Tully said indifferently.

"The . . ." Henry found himself half standing.

The moneylender leaned back with a swively creak that crawled up Henry's spine. "I've run into a little recession, you might call it. You know? Overextended. So I'm calling my loans in. Sorry."

"But when I took the loan, Mr. Tully, you assured me—"

"Now don't give me that." Tully flicked some papers from the folder, his murderous eyes suddenly intent. "There's a demand clause in these notes, friend. Want to read it over?"

Henry did not try to focus. He knew what the fine print said. But last year he would have signed anything; he had borrowed the limit from legitimate loan companies and Tully had been his last resort.

Tully lit a big cigar. "You've got forty-eight hours to hand me a certified check for $490."

Henry put his finger on the tic. "I haven't got it, Mr. Tully."

"Borrow it."

"I can't. I can't get any more loans. I have a crippled child —the operations, a therapist who comes in every day—"

The moneylender picked up a letter opener with a sharp point and began to clean his fingernails. "Look, Witter, you got your troubles and I got mine. Be here Thursday night nine o'clock with your check, or I take action."

Henry stumbled out.

Ellery was watching "The Late Show" on TV Thursday night when his doorbell rang. He opened the door and a woman with a worn cloth coat thrown over her housedress fell into his arms. Her eyes were wild.

"Mr. Queen? I'm Claire Witter, Mrs. Henry Witter. I live in the neighborhood—left the children with a neighbor—ran all the way. They say you help people in trouble—"

"Get your breath, Mrs. Witter," Ellery said, supporting her. "Just what kind of trouble are you in?"

"My husband's just been picked up by the police. I understand an Inspector Queen is in charge. He's your father, I'm told. But Henry didn't do it, Mr. Queen—"

"What didn't Henry do?"

"Kill that moneylender! They've taken Henry to the office where Tully's body was found. I don't know what to do." And Claire Witter sobbed like a little girl.

"Now, now," Ellery said. "I'll get my hat."

The Inspector had invited Ellery to trail along when the homicide call came in about 10:30, and Ellery had pleaded fatigue; so the old man was surprised when his son showed up not two hours later.

"I'm representing Mrs. Witter," Ellery told him. "What's the charge against her husband?"

"Suspicion of murder."

"As pat as all that, dad?" Ellery glanced around the crowded office. He had left Claire Witter in the hall in the care of a patrolman. "Is that my client?"

A white-faced man with clerical shoulders was leaning against the wall, his eyes shut, and with Sergeant Velie's beef between him and the possibly tempting open window. Nearby huddled a frowsy old lady, a dumpy woman in a smart suit, and an Italian-looking man with a big gray mustache.

Inspector Queen nodded. "The one next to Velie. And don't tell me Witter doesn't look the type."

"He doesn't."

"Just goes to show. It's Witter, all right."

The basket crew were crating the remains of Mr. Tully. Ellery glimpsed the back of a tan jacket splattered with blood.

"I don't see the weapon. Knife?"

"Tully's letter opener. We couldn't seem to raise a print, so we sent it down to the lab."

Ellery looked around at the bare room, the bare floor. "Those empty desk and file drawers were found open, the way they are now?"

"Nothing's been changed or removed except the letter opener. By the way, the heat was on Tully for a usury charge and he must have got wind of it. He was getting set to skip. Anyway, here's the rundown. Prouty says Tully was knifed tonight between 8:30 and 9:30—"

The Inspector paused; Mr. Tully was leaving. Ellery hoped Claire Witter would be crying on the patrolman's shoulder when the basket passed her in the hall. There was blood on it.

"Three people entered this office during that hour," the Inspector resumed. "That dumpy woman next to the man with the mustache—her name is Mrs. Lester. Mr. Mustache came next—he's a barber named Dominini. Finally, Witter."

"Who's the old lady beside Mrs. Lester?"

"The cleaning woman of the building. She found the body." The Inspector raised his voice. "Mrs. Bogan?"

The old woman shuffled forward on her shapeless shoes. She still had her work-apron on and a dust cloth bound around her lifeless white hair.

"Tell your story again, Mrs. Bogan."

"Couple minutes after ten I comes in here to clean." She had badly fitted false teeth, and her words came bubbling and hissing out like water from a rusty faucet. "What do I see but Mr. Tully laying with his face on the desk and a knife sticking outen his back. There was all blood . . ." Her bleary eyes rolled. But there was nothing on the desk now.

"Did you touch anything, Mrs. Bogan?" Ellery asked.

"Me? I run out yelling me head off. Found a cop in the street and that's all I know, Mister. I'll be seeing that knife sticking outen his back in me dreams."

"You didn't hear anything—a fight, an argument—between half-past eight and half-past nine?"

"I wasn't on this floor then. I was cleaning two floors down."

"Mrs. Lester," Inspector Queen called out.

The dumpy woman in the smart suit blanched under her heavy makeup. She was well into her forties, her hair hennaed to a screaming red, her figure fighting a corset. She kept biting her lips, but Ellery saw under her nervousness the expression of chronic restlessness so often worn by women with too little to do.

"You were one of Tully's victims, too?" he asked her.

"Don't tell my husband," Mrs. Lester said in a rapid-fire falsetto. "He'd kick me out, no kidding. I had to get a loan on the q.t., see, because of—well, a bunch of us girls have a little afternoon poker club. We started out sociable, but I don't know, the limit kept getting higher . . . The thing is, I went into the hole for a lot of money, mostly to that Mrs. Carson. If my husband Phil knew—he's a nut against gambling . . . Anyway, she says if I don't pay up she'll go to Phil. So I took a $600 loan from this shark Tully."

"And Tully called the loan in, Mrs. Lester?"

The woman's gloved hands began to writhe. "He said I had to pay off the whole thing by half-past eight tonight. Meantime I'd lost more—I swear to God those harpies play with marked cards! So I came here at half-past eight and I hand Tully two hundred dollars—all I could scrape up between what I could sneak off my household money and a ring I hocked that I told Phil I lost. But Tully says nothing doing.

So I start begging him to give me more time, and all he does, the rat, is sit here emptying desk drawers and throwing away papers and ignoring me like I was dirt!"

"Why was he doing that, Mrs. Lester?"

"How should I know? He takes my money and says either I have the other four hundred for him by tomorrow morning or he goes to my husband. I left him still tearing up papers."

"Alive, of course," Ellery smiled.

"Are you kidding? Say, you don't think—" Her bloated eyes began to look terrified.

"Mr. Dominini," Inspector Queen cut in.

The barber bounded forward in bitter excitement. It took a great many haircuts and shaves to keep his ten children in *pasta* and shoe leather, he exclaimed. He had a small neighborhood shop that could accommodate only so many. The neighborhood had run down, lots of poor people had moved in, Mr. Dominini said, and even with the higher prices barbers had to charge these days things got worse and worse. Finally, he had faced the possible loss of his shop.

"I go to bank, bank say Dominini no good risk no more," the barber shouted, brandishing his clean hairy hands. "What can I do? I go to Tully, the blood suck'!"

For a year he had managed to meet Tully's usurious interest charges. Then, on Tuesday, the loan shark had phoned him and demanded payment in full by Thursday night. He named a quarter to nine as the deadline.

"Where Dominini get fifteen hundred dollar?" the mustachioed barber cried. "I bring him five hundred sixty-five, it's a best I can do. He say, Dominini, that's a no good. I say okay, Mr. Tully, you run barber shop, I work for you. He call me bad name, take my money, say get out, I sue you. Couple hour later, the policeman he pick me up. For what? My wife she cry, *bambini* run under bed . . . I no kill Tully!"

"Then he was alive when you left this office tonight, Mr. Dominini?" Ellery said. "That's your story?"

"It's a true!"

"Clearing Mrs. Lester," Inspector Queen murmured.

Ellery frowned. "What was Tully doing, if anything," he asked the barber, "while you were here?"

"Like a that lady say. He take a things out of file cabinet. Tear up paper, folder."

"Bringing us," the Inspector said, "to Henry Witter."

Sergeant Velie had to assist Henry forward. The bookkeeper sank into the chair, his tic working overtime. Suddenly his nostrils expanded. He looked up. Ellery was lighting a cigaret.

"Might I have one?" Henry asked. "I've run out."

"Sure. No, that's all right. Keep the pack."

"Oh, no—"

"I have another, Mr. Witter."

"Thanks. Thanks a million." Henry inhaled hungrily. "I should have cut them out long ago." He puffed and puffed.

"Mr. Witter, you found Tully alive at nine?"

"Oh, yes," Henry said.

"Alive and alone?"

Henry nodded.

"Clearing Dominini," the Inspector murmured. "Neat?"

"Even gaudy," Ellery murmured back. "Tell me just what happened, Mr. Witter, after you got here."

Henry lit a fresh cigaret from the butt of the old one, looked around, hesitated, then tossed the smoldering butt into the wastebasket.

"I told Tully I hadn't been able to raise the money. I said, you can do what you want, Mr. Tully, sue me, have me arrested, beaten up, killed, it won't do you any good, you can't get blood from a stone. He kept sitting there behind the desk tearing up papers and records as if he didn't hear me. But he was paying attention, all right." Henry gulped in a lungful of smoke. "Because as soon as I got through he started to chew me out. What he called me—"

Henry choked over the smoke. After a moment Ellery said, "Yes, Mr. Witter?"

"I never raised my hand in anger to anybody in my life. But Tully said some things to me no man could take. Real nasty things. And while he was saying them I kept getting sorer and sorer." Henry's tic was hopping around now like a flea. "I thought of all the months we'd scrimped to pay him his blood money and at the same time pay for the medical care my little girl Jody needs so maybe some day she'll walk again. I thought of the stockings my wife couldn't buy, the baseball cards my Eddie couldn't collect, the complaints we didn't make to the Health Department about the cockroaches because the landlord might get mad and somehow chisel us out of the apartment and we'd have to rent another place at a bigger rent . . . I thought of a lot of things like that, and then I leaned over the desk and let Tully have it."

"With the paper knife?" Ellery asked gently.

"Huh?" Henry Witter came back to the present. "No, with this." Henry made a skinny fist and looked at it. "I pasted him one right on the button. Socko!" The memory of it gave him a momentary pleasure; a spark of life came into his eyes. "I didn't know I could hit that hard. He went out like a light."

"How did he fall, Mr. Witter?"

"On his face on the desk. I certainly was surprised. But I felt better, too. So then I walked out."

"Leaving Tully unconscious but alive?"

"Sure. He was breathing like a walrus."

"Did you notice anyone in the hall, or downstairs?"

"Just the night man mopping in the lobby."

"And that's how we know," Inspector Queen said to his son, "that nobody else entered the building between Witter's leaving and Mrs. Bogan's finding the body. The porter saw Witter come and go, and he was in the lobby working the whole time afterward. Yes, Velie?"

The Sergeant, who had been summoned into the hall, came back to rumble into the Inspector's ear.

"That cinches it," the Inspector snapped. "The lab's found three partially smeared prints on Tully's letter knife. One is Tully's. The other two have been identified, Witter, as yours."

Henry Witter sat there with his mouth open. But then he yelped as the cigaret burned his fingers. He flung it into the wastebasket and covered his face with his hands. Ellery, fearing a fire, walked over to the basket, but he saw that it was empty except for the two butts.

"So, Witter," Inspector Queen began.

"Hold it, dad." Ellery stooped over Henry. "Mr. Witter, while you were seated here across the desk from Tully, did you happen to handle the letter knife?"

Henry looked up dully. "I must have, if my fingerprints are on it. I don't remember. But I didn't use it on Tully. I'd remember that. God, yes. Don't you believe me, Inspector?"

"No," Inspector Queen said. "No, Witter, I don't. Take my advice and come clean. Maybe the D.A. would consent to a lesser plea—"

"Maybe the D.A. would, but I won't," Ellery said. "My client will plead not guilty."

Sergeant Velie remarked with some bitterness to no one in particular, "And the beauty of it is, he does it all with his little sleeves rolled up."

The Inspector's glance at the Sergeant was a terrible thing. "How come, Ellery?"

"Because they aren't here," Ellery said, waving vaguely.

"Because *what* aren't here?"

"The papers."

"*What* papers?"

"Look," Ellery said. "Mrs. Lester, Dominini, Witter—all

three say Tully was cleaning out his desk and file, throwing away papers and records. You told me, dad, that nothing has been removed from this office except Tully's letter knife. Yet the file and desk drawers are cleaned out, the floor is bare, there's nothing on the desk—*and the wastebasket is empty.* I ask you: Where are all the papers and records Tully was throwing out?"

His father looked as if he had been struck by lightning. He turned toward the old cleaning woman cowering in her corner, but Ellery was there before him. "You'd been inside this office earlier tonight than you claimed, Mrs. Bogan," Ellery was saying "—right after Witter left, in fact. And you found Tully just recovering from Witter's haymaker."

The old woman blinked.

"You owed Tully money, too, didn't you, Mrs. Bogan? And he put the screws on you tonight as well, while you were cleaning his office—right? You'd already emptied the wastebasket and taken the contents outside when you killed him. By the way, how did you come to owe Tully money?"

The old woman blinked and blinked. Finally she touched her liverish old lips with her old tongue, and she said, "Me boy Jim. Jim's a three-times loser. Next time he gets sent up, it's for life. And then what's he do but hook a wad outen the till in the garage where he's working. The boss says he won't send Jimmy up if I pays back the money, so I borries it offen Tully . . . I paid him his interest faithful.

"But tonight Tully says he wants all the money or he'll have me pinched. I didn't care about meself, I've had it, but if I wasn't around to keep an eye on Jim . . . I had me cleaning gloves on . . . I sees the knife on Tully's desk . . . I was in back of him . . ." Her old face settled, but it was hard to tell whether the lines told of remorse, resignation, or indifference. But then she said, "Now who'll be keeping me Jimmy out of trouble?"

Inspector Queen said furiously, "Maybe you, mother, maybe you. Just tell that story of yours to a jury."

When they had taken the old lady out, Ellery nudged Henry Witter, whose mouth was open. "You still here? Don't you know there's a lady waiting for you in the hall?"

"Claire." Henry hauled himself out of the chair.

"Oh, and you might remember," Ellery said severely, "— I'm thinking of your little girl, Mr. Witter—that miracles do happen."

Henry shook himself like a dog coming out of a mud hole. "You bet, Mr. Queen," he said. "Thanks for reminding me."

Q.B.I.: QUEEN'S BUREAU OF INVESTIGATION

Gambling Dept.:
The Lonely Bride

Certain things should come together: for example, one shoe and another or one love bird and another. So when Ellery observed on the fourth finger of his beautiful young petitioner's left hand a circlet of entwined golden roses which had not yet lost the bright dew of the jeweler's garden, he grasped at once the missing complement: a groom, probably young and almost certainly a fool or a rascal. Only folly or worse explained a newlywed husband who left such a bloom untended.

Her name was Shelley, she confessed in the Queen apartment, she was a New Yorker from Evanston, a model by profession, and the fellow having seen her laminated in four colors on a magazine cover had pursued her with such wolfish purpose that she found herself one day in the City Clerk's office being made Mrs. Jimmy Browne. For their honeymoon they had cruised the world, madly rich in love, and lesser goods, too, for young Mr. Browne seemed bottomlessly supplied with the vulgar commodity by which lovers satisfy their appetites for giving, and he was insatiable. On their return to New York three days before, he had set her up in a princely furnished suite at L'Aiglon Towers, excused himself "for a few hours on a little business matter," kissed her passionately,

around inside the amphitheater of the imitation Italian fireplace. "She said a book."

"I know what she said," mumbled Ellery; but while Cookie devoured half a dozen ladyfingers he examined each *objet d'amour* painstakingly to convince himself that no crevice or secret recess concealed the two images of Secretary Chase.

Afterward, Ellery looked thoughtful. He removed his jacket.

At 4:06 the eminent sleuth raised a dusty nose to announce: "There is positively no book in this apartment, not so much as a memo or telephone book. And there are no ten-thousand-dollar bills, either. Still, Shelley said . . ." And he threw himself on the sofa and closed his eyes . . .

"No change yet," said Jimmy Browne hollowly, dropping the telephone. Cookie reached into his bulging pocket and Jimmy blanched. But the flipper came out clutching a bag of coconut macaroons.

At 4:31 Ellery raised his head from the angular couch on which he labored. "I've decided," he said, "that something is missing from this room."

"Sure, twenty grand. *Stop munching, you cow!*"

At 4:53 the telephone screamed. Cookie almost dropped a Nabisco. It was the hospital. Mrs. Browne was still unconscious, but the prognosis was suddenly good. She would live. Jimmy promised again. "But what good will a dead husband do her? Queen, I was leveling—I'll look for that job." Wildly he eyed the door. "Just find my dough!"

"Big T's dough, I believe," said Cookie courteously, and when his hand emerged this time it grasped an inedible roscoe, which he began to examine with earnestness.

And then, at 5:13, Ellery sprang from his bed of pain. "I was right!"

"About what?"

"There is something missing from this room, Jimmy. Now I know where Shelley hid those bills!"

"Jimmy," said Ellery, "certain things are inseparable. Shoes, for instance. Love birds." He took Shelley's Tyrolean bride from the bookshelf; the marble base was heavy and he hefted it smilingly. "What was missing was this bas-relief lady's husband. *Whoever heard of a bride without a groom?*"

Jimmy stared. "Say. There *were* a pair. But where's the other one?"

Ellery hefted the little lady again and then he hurled her, straight and true, at Cookie Napoli, who was thoughtfully edging toward the door. The Tyrolean bride caught Big T's triggerman on the chin; Cookie landed on the floor, Jimmy landed on Cookie, and Ellery landed on the roscoe. "When we found Cookie outside your door we assumed he was waiting. Actually, he was leaving. But he had to brazen it out . . . Ah, a sack of fudge squares, and what's this in his other pocket? The missing bridegroom. Felt's loose, metal bas-relief is hollow, and I believe—yes—you'll find your ten-thousand-dollar bills inside. Cookie heard us coming and pocketed the works for future reference."

"But she said—Shelley said—" Mr. Browne spluttered as he tore at the shell of the metal bridegroom "—Shelley said she hid it in a book."

"Bas-relief—meaning a flat back—attached to a marble base with a felt bottom—and they come in pairs. Poor Shelley passed out before she could finish her sentence. What your wife meant to say," said Mr. Queen, grasping the roscoe more firmly as Cookie stirred, "was 'In a book*end*.'"

Spy Dept.: Mystery
at the Library of Congress

Ellery responded to Inspector Terence Fineberg's invitation with pleasure. Fineberg, in charge of the Central Office, was one of Inspector Queen's ancient beat-buddies, and he used to slip Ellery candy bars. He detested amateur detectives, so the old mink must be desperate.

"Park it," Inspector Fineberg said, blowing hot and cold. "You know Inspector Pete Santoria of the Narcotics Squad?"

Ellery nodded to the stone-jawed Narcotics man.

"We'll skip the protocol, Ellery," Fineberg went on, gnashing his dentures. "Calling you in wasn't our idea. The big brass thought this case could use your screwb—your God-given talents."

"I'm ever at the beck of the law enforcement arm," Ellery said kindly, "especially when it's grasping at straws. You may fire when ready, Finey."

"The buck," Fineberg shouted to Inspector Santoria, "is yours."

Santoria said in tooth-sucking tones, "We got a line on a new dope ring, Queen. The junk is coming in, we think, from France, and in kilo lots. New York is the distribution depot.

None of the lower echelons knows any of the others except the few in immediate contact. We want the big boy on the New York end. That this gang aren't regulars is about all we know for sure."

"Of course they're no regulars," the Central Office head grumbled. "Who ever heard of a regular dope-running crumbum who could read?"

"Read?" Ellery came to a point like a bird-dog. "Read what, Finey?"

"Books, for gossakes!"

"Don't tell me we authors are now being blamed for the narcotics traffic, too," Ellery said coldly. "How do books come into this?"

"Using 'em as a code!" Terence Fineberg implored the ceiling to witness. "An information-passing operation is going on down in Washington that's an intermediate step between shipment and delivery. The Federal Bureau of Narcotics got on the trail of the D.C. members of the ring—two of 'em, anyway—and they're both being watched."

"One of the two," Inspector Santoria took it up, "is a colorless little shnook named Balcom who works for a Washington travel agency. He used to be a high school English teacher. The other—a girl named Norma Shuffing—is employed at the Library of Congress."

"The Library's being used as the contact rendezvous?"

"Yes. Balcom's job is to pass along the information as to when, where, and how a new shipment is coming into New York. The contact to whom he has to pass the information is identified for Balcom by the Shuffing girl. They play it cool —a different contact is used every time."

Ellery shrugged. "All you have to do is spot one as the Shuffing girl points him out to Balcom—"

"Yes, sir, Mr. Queen," the Narcotics chief said, sounding like the Witch in *Hansel and Gretel*. "Want a go at it?"

"Just what takes place?" Ellery asked intently.

Inspector Fineberg's glance quelled Santoria. "Balcom visits the Library only when the girl is on duty—she works out of the main desk filling call slips and bringing the books onto the floor. Balcom takes either Desk One Forty-seven or, if that's occupied, the nearest one that's vacant. When Shuffing spies him she brings him some books conforming to slips filled out by her in advance. It's the titles of the books that tip him off—she never communicates with him in any other way."

"Titles," Ellery said, nuzzling the word. "What does Balcom do?"

"He looks the books over, then takes an easy gander around his immediate neighborhood. And that's all. After that he just sits there reading, doesn't take his eyes off his books, till closing time, when he gets up and goes home."

"The Library bit is just so Balcom can identify the messenger," Inspector Santoria said. "The actual passage of the information is made at a different meet."

"But if Balcom's being watched—"

"He works for a travel agency, I told you! Any idea how many people he comes in contact with daily?"

"We figure it works like this, Ellery," the Central Office head explained. "After a session at the Library—the next morning, say—the messenger that this Norma Shuffing identified for Balcom through the book titles shows up at the travel agency as a customer. Balcom recognizes him and passes him a legitimate ticket envelope, only it contains not just plane or railroad tickets, but the dope shipment info, too."

"And if you could spot one of these contacts—"

"We could track Balcom's message to its destination. That would be Big Stuff himself, who's sure as hell covered behind a smart front here in New York."

A contact and shipment, Ellery learned, occurred about once every ten days. The Federals had set up their first stake-out a month before, and at that time Miss Shuffing had brought three books to Balcom's desk.

"What were they?"

Inspector Santoria fished a report from a folder. "Steve Allen's *The Funny Men*, Count Leo Tolstoy's *War and Peace*, and Sigmund Freud's *Interpretation of Dreams*."

"Lovely!" Ellery murmured. "Allen, Tolstoy, Freud . . . Well." He seemed disappointed. "It's simple enough. A kindergarten acrostic—"

"Sure," Terence Fineberg retorted. "F for Freud, A for Allen, T for Tolstoy. F-A-T. There was a three-hundred-pound character sitting near Balcom."

"The trouble was," Santoria said, "the Feds and we weren't on to the system that first time, and by the time we'd figured it out the fat guy had already got his info from Balcom and taken off."

"What about the second contact?"

"Three books again. Chekhov's *The Cherry Orchard*, George R. Stewart's *Fire*, and Ben Hecht's *Actor's Blood*."

"C-S-H. No acrostic there. Changed the system . . ." Ellery frowned. "Must be in the titles—something in common . . . Was there an American Indian sitting near Balcom on that visit? Or someone with red hair?"

"Quick, isn't he, Pete?" Inspector Fineberg asked sourly. "Yeah, we saw that—cherries, fire, blood are all red. It was an old dame with dyed red hair sitting a couple seats from Balcom. Only again we doped it out too late to cover the actual contact. The third time we missed clean."

"Ah, couldn't find the common denominator."

"What common denominator?" Santoria asked angrily. "You got to have at least two items for that!"

"There was only *one* book the third time?"

"Right! I still say the doll got suspicious and never brought the other books. But do you think the brass would listen to me? No, they got to call in a screwb—an expert!"

"The thing is, Ellery," Inspector Fineberg said, "we do have evidence that a third shipment was picked up, which means a contact *was* made after that one-book deal."

"They did it some other way, Terence!" Santoria snapped.

"Sure, Pete, sure," Fineberg said soothingly. "I go along with you. Only the brass don't. They want Brains working on this. Who are we to reason why?"

"What was the book?" Ellery asked.

"Rudyard Kipling's *The Light That Failed*."

Santoria growled. "We waited around the whole damn afternoon while people came and went—what a turnover they get down there—and our boy Balcom sits there at Desk One Forty-seven reading the Kipling book from cover to cover like he was enjoying it!"

"The Light That Failed was about a man who went blind. Was there someone in the vicinity wearing dark glasses, or immersed in a volume of Braille?"

"No blind people, no cheaters, no Braille, no nothing."

Ellery mused. "Do you have a written report of that visit to the Library?"

Santoria dug out another folder. Ellery glanced through it. It was a detailed account of the third Balcom-Shuffing contact, complete with descriptions of suspects, unclassified incidents, and so on. Ellery emerged from this rubble bearing a nugget.

"Of course," he said gently. "The one book by Kipling was all Balcom needed that day. A saintly-looking old gent wearing a clerical collar was consulting a card catalogue within view of Balcom and absently filled his pipe. He was flipping the wheel of his pocket lighter—flipped it unsuccessfully several times, it says here, boys—when a guard walked over and stopped him. The old fellow apologized for his absent-mindedness, put the lighter and pipe away, and went on consulting the index cards. *The Light That Failed.*"

"Lemme see that!" Fineberg snatched the folder, red in the face. "Pete," he howled, "how the devil did we miss that?"

"We thought sure there'd be more books, Terence," Inspector Santoria stammered. "And the old guy was a preacher—"

"The old guy was a phony! Look, Ellery, maybe you can help us at that. We've been slow on the uptake—books yet! If on the next meet you could be sitting near Balcom and spot the contact man right away— How about it."

"You couldn't keep me out of this with a court order, Finey," Ellery assured him. "What's more, it won't cost the City of New York a plugged subway token—I'll pay my own expenses to Washington. Can you arrange it with the Feds?"

Inspector Fineberg arranged it with the Feds, and on Monday of the following week Ellery was snugged down one desk behind and to the right of Desk 147 in the main reading room of the venerable gray Renaissance building east of the Capitol in downtown Washington. One of his fellow stakeout men, a balding Federal Narcotics agent named Hauck who looked like a senior accountant in a wholesale drygoods firm, was parked in the outermost concentric circle of desks, near the entrance; they could signal each other by a half turn of the head. Another Federal agent and Inspector Santoria lounged around outside making like camera bugs.

Ellery's desk was loaded with reference books, for he was being an Author in Search of Material, a role he had often played at the Library of Congress in earnest.

He had filed his slips at the main desk with Norma Shuffing, whose photo—along with Balcom's—he had studied at the Federal Bureau. When she brought the books to his desk he was able to get a close look. Tense and sad-looking, she was a pretty, dark-eyed girl who had been at some pains to camouflage her prettiness. Ellery wondered how she had come to be mixed up in an international dope operation; she could not have been more than twenty years old.

The little travel agent, Balcom, did not appear that day. Ellery had not expected him to, for the Federal men had said that Balcom visited the Library only on his days off, which were unpredictable. Today he was reported swamped at the office by a tidal wave of travel orders.

"But it's got to be soon, Queen," Inspector Santoria said Monday night in Ellery's room at the Hotel Mayflower. "Tomorrow's the eleventh day since the last meet, and they've never gone this long before."

"Balcom may not be able to get away from his office."

"He'll manage it," Agent Hauck said grimly.

Early the next morning Ellery's phone rang. It was Santoria. "I just got the word from Hauck. It's today."

"How's Balcom managing it?"

"He's reported out sick. Better get on over to the Library."

Norma Shuffing was bringing Ellery an armful of books when a little man with mousy eyes and mousy hair, dressed in a mousy business suit, pat-patted past Ellery's desk and slipped into the seat of Desk 147. Ellery did not need Hauck's pencil-to-nose signal to identify the newcomer. It was Balcom.

The Shuffing girl passed Desk 147 without a glance. She placed Ellery's books softly before him and returned to her station. Ellery began to turn pages.

It was fascinating to watch them. Balcom and the girl might have inhabited different planets. Balcom stared at the encircling walls, the very picture of a man waiting. Not once did he look toward the main desk. There, her back to him, the pretty girl was quietly busy.

The reading room began to fill.

Ellery continued to study the two of them from above his book. Balcom had his dainty hands clasped on his desk now; he seemed to be dozing. Norma Shuffing was fetching books, working on the floor dozens of feet away.

A quarter of an hour passed.

Ellery sneaked an inventory of the readers in the vicinity. To Balcom's left sat a buxom woman in a smart strawberry silk suit; she wore bifocals and was raptly reading a volume of industrial reports.

To Balcom's right a very large man with wrestler's shoulders and no hair was absorbed in a volume on African lovebirds.

Beyond the bird-lover a sloppily dressed Latin who looked like Fidel Castro's double was making secretive notes from some ancient *National Geographics*.

Near the Cuban-looking man sat a thin elongated lady with a lavender-rinse hairdo who reminded Ellery of Miss Hildegarde Withers; she was intent on the *Congressional Record*.

Also in the neighborhood were a scowling young priest who was leafing through a book on demonology; a Man of Distinction with a gray crewcut and an egg-spattered necktie who was frankly dozing; and a young lady with hearing-aid eyeglasses and some blue ink on one nostril who was copying something from a book on naval ordnance as if her life depended on it.

Suddenly the Shuffing girl started up the aisle. She was carrying a thick, oversized book.

Ellery turned a page. Was this it?

It was!

Miss Shuffing paused at Desk 147, placed the book deftly before Balcom, and walked away.

Balcom unclasped his little hands and opened the book to the title page.

The Complete Shakespeare.

The Complete Shakespeare?

Balcom began to idle through the volume. He made no attempt to survey his fellow readers.

Shakespeare . . . Some relevant quotation? Not likely, with thousands to cull.

Ellery concentrated.

Plays? A playwright? An actor? Nothing about anyone in the vicinity suggested the theater. Moreover, Balcom seemed obviously to be waiting.

Ten minutes later Miss Shuffing silently laid another book on Desk 147 and as silently took herself off.

This time Balcom reached for the book with something like eagerness. Ellery craned.

Shaw . . . Shaw's *Man and Superman.*

A playwright again! But how could you make an instant identification of a playwright—or an actor, for the matter? Ellery glanced about under the pretext of stretching. No one within eyeshot was even reading a play.

Shakespeare—Shaw. Initials? S, S. *SS!* An ex-Nazi Storm Trooper? The big bald wrestlerish character who was interested in African lovebirds? Possibly, but how could anyone be sure? It had to be something Balcom could interpret with certainty at a glance. Besides, the fellow didn't look Teutonic, but Slavic.

Shakespeare, Shaw . . . English literature. An Englishman? No one Ellery could see looked English, although any of them might be. Besides, Shaw was really Irish.

Man and Superman? Somehow that didn't fit in with Shakespeare.

Ellery shook his head. What the deuce was the girl trying to convey to Balcom?

Balcom was now reading Shaw with concentration. But then he had to keep doing something. Was he waiting for another volume? Or would he soon look around and spot the contact?

If he does, Ellery thought with exasperation, he's a better man than I am!

But Balcom did not look up from the Shaw book. He was

showing no curiosity about his neighbors, so Ellery decided
that he was expecting another book . . .

Yes, a third book was coming!

The Shuffing girl placed it on Desk 147. Ellery could
barely contain himself.

He read the title almost simultaneously with Balcom, bless-
ing his sharp eyesight.

Personal Memoirs of U.S. Grant.

Blam went his theories! Shakespeare and Shaw, play-
wrights; Grant, a military man. S, S, now G. One Englishman, one Irishman, one American.

What did it all add up to?

Ellery couldn't think of a thing. He could feel Agent
Hauck's eyes boring critical holes in his back.

And the minutes went bucketing by.

He now studied Balcom with ferocity. Did the three books
mean anything to *him?* Not yet. Balcom was in trouble, too,
as he pretended to glance through the Grant autobiography.
Puzzlement showed in every slightest movement.

Shakespeare . . . Shaw . . . General Grant . . .

Balcom had it!

He was now looking around casually, his gaze never linger-
ing, as if one glimpse was all he needed.

Ellery struggled with panic. Any moment Balcom's contact might get up and leave, knowing Balcom had spotted
him. People were constantly coming and going; it would be
impossible to identify the right one without the clue conveyed
by the books. Ellery could already hear Inspector Santoria's
horse laugh . . .

And then—O blessed!—he had it, too!

Ellery rose. He plucked his hat from the desk, strolled up
the aisle past Agent Hauck, who had chewed his pencil eraser
to crumbs, and went out into the Washington sunshine. Inspector Santoria and the other Federal man were seated in an
unmarked car now, and Ellery slipped into the rear seat.

"Well?" the Federal man demanded. The Feds had been
polite, but skeptical, over the New York brass's inspiration.

"Wait for Hauck."

Agent Hauck came out two minutes later. He paused near
the car to light a cigaret, and Ellery said, "Get set for the
tail. The contact is sitting two seats over to Balcom's right in
the same row. He's the sloppy little Cuban type."

"Afternoon, Finey," Ellery said on Friday of that
week. "Don't tell me. You're stumped again."

"No, no, haha, sit down, my boy," Inspector Terence Fineberg said cordially. "You're ace-high around here! Thought you'd like to know Pete Santoria collared Big Stuff two hours ago in the act of taking possession of a shipment of H. The Feds are out right now picking up Balcom and the girl. By the way, that little Havana number who led us to him was never closer to Cuba than an El Stinko cigar. He's a pool-room punk name of Harry Hummelmayer from the Red Hook section of Brooklyn."

Ellery nodded unenthusiastically. The spirit of the chase had long since left him. "Well, Finey, congratulations and all that. Was there something else? I have a date with four walls and an empty typewriter."

"Wait, Ellery, for gossakes! I've been going Nutsville trying to figure out a connection between Shakespeare, Shaw, and old man Grant. Even knowing the contact was Hummelmayer, I can't see what the three have in common."

"With Hummelmayer looking like Fidel Castro?" Ellery reached over the desk and, gripping Inspector Fineberg's knotty chin firmly, waggled it. "Beards, Finey, beards."

Spy Dept.: Dead Ringer

The hush-hush man's name was Storke, and Ellery had once before worked with him on a case involving the security of the United States. So when Storke showed up out of no-where and said, "Scene of the crime first, the rundown later," Ellery dropped what he was doing and reached for his hat without a question.

Storke drove him downtown, chatting pleasantly, parked on one of the meandering side streets below Park Row in a space that was magically unoccupied, and strolled Ellery over to a thin shop-front with a dusty window bearing the crabbed legend: *M. Merrilees Monk, Tobacconist, Est. 1897.*

Two young men who looked like Wall Street clerks on their dinner hour lounged outside, puffing on pipes. There was no sign of a police uniform.

"This must be a big one," murmured Ellery; and he preceded Storke into the shop.

It was as aged-looking inside as out, narrow and poorly lighted, with walls of some musty dark wood, Victorian fix-tures, and a gas-jet for lighting cigarets and cigars. Every-thing was pungent with tobacco.

In the deeps of the little shop, near the curtained doorway to a rear room, stood a venerable wooden Indian, his original splendor bedraggled to a sprinkle of color here and there; most of him was naked pitted wood.

The Indian appeared forlorn, whereas the dead man who lay jammed between the counter and the shelves looked outraged, for he had suffered cruelly at the hands not of time but of an assassin. His head and face resembled a jellied mash.

Curiously, his dead arms embraced a large squarish canister apparently used for the storage of pipe tobacco, for it was labeled MIX C and obviously came from a row of similar canisters on one of the upper shelves behind the cluttered counter.

"He was attacked from behind at this point," Ellery said to Storke, indicating a stiffening puddle at the feet of the wooden Indian, "probably as he was going into the back room for something. The killer must have left him for dead; but he wasn't dead, because this blood trail goes from the Indian all the way around and behind the counter to where he's lying now.

"The picture is unmistakable: When the killer left, this man somehow—don't ask me how!—managed to drag himself to that particular spot, and in spite of his frightful injuries reached up to that tobacco can and took it down from that empty space on the shelf before he died."

"That's the way I read it, too," said Storke.

"May I handle the canister?"

"Everything's been processed."

Ellery took the canister from the dead man, who seemed disposed to resist, and pried off the lid. The canister was empty. He borrowed a powerful magnifier from the hush-hush man. After a moment he put the lens down.

"This canister never contained tobacco, Storke. Not a shred or speck is visible under the glass, even at the seams."

Storke said nothing; and Ellery turned to the shelves. Nine canisters remained on the shelf from which the dead man had taken the MIX C can. They were labeled MONK'S SPECIAL, BARTLEBY MIXTURE, SUPERBA BLEND, MIX A, MIX B, (and here was the space where the MIX C can must have stood), KENTUCKY LONG CUT, VIRGINIA CRIMP, LORD CAVENDISH, and MANHATTAN MIX.

"Those nine are *not* empty," said Storke, reading Ellery's mind. "Each contains what it's labeled."

Ellery squatted by the corpse. It was enveloped in a knee-length tobacconist's gown in the British fashion—a rather surprisingly muscular body of a man in his early 40s with what must once have been a sandy-fringed bald pate and sharp Anglican features.

"This, I take it, was M. Merrilees Monk," Ellery said. "Or his lineal descendant."

"Wrong on both counts," Storke replied bitterly. "He was one of our topflight operatives, and don't mention him in the same breath with Monk. As far as we know, Monk's grandfather and father were respectable tobacconists, but the incumbent is a turncoat who ran this shop as a drop for foreign agents to pick up and pass along messages, stolen material, and so on.

"We got on to Monk only recently. We put the shop under round-the-clock surveillance, but we weren't able to spot any known enemy agent entering or leaving.

"Then we got what we thought was a break. One of our Seattle men, Hartman, turned out to be a dead ringer for this Monk rat. So we brought Hartman on from the Coast, put him through an intensive training course on Monk, then took Monk into custody in the middle of one night, substituted Hartman, and called off our outside men to leave Hartman a clear field in the shop. He knew the risk he was running."

"And it caught up with him. Dead ringer is right." Ellery brooded over the battered U.S. agent's remains. "How long had he been playing the part of Monk?"

"Fifteen days. And no one turned up, Hartman was positive. He spent his spare time in the stockroom out back, microfilming the shop's ledger, which lists the names of hundreds of Monk's customers, each with an account number and address. Good thing he did, too, because the killer's made off with the ledger.

"Just this morning," Storke went on somberly, "Hartman phoned in that he'd found out two of the listed customers were foreign agents—exactly how we'll probably never know, because he didn't get a chance to explain. A customer walked in at that moment and he had to hang up. By the time we felt it safe to make contact with him tonight, he'd been murdered. One or both of the agents must have paid a visit to the shop as Hartman was closing up and spotted him as a ringer."

"They probably had a signal Hartman missed." Ellery stared at the empty tobacco canister. "Storke, why have you called me in on this?"

"You're looking at the reason."

"The MIX C can? It was almost certainly Monk's repository for whatever was delivered to him to be passed along. But if it contained any spy material at the time Hartman was assaulted, Storke, his killer or killers took it and blew."

"Exactly," said the hush-hush man. "That means Hartman made that superhuman effort in order to take down an *empty* can. Why was his last act to call our attention to the can?"

"Obviously he was trying to tell you something."

"Of course," said Storke impatiently. "But what? That's what we can't figure out, Ellery, and that's why I called you in. Any notions?"

"Yes," said Ellery. "He was telling you who the foreign agents are."

Storke was not given to displays of emotion, but on this occasion astonishment slackened his solid jaw and widened his shrewd eyes.

"Well, he hasn't told me a damned thing," the hush-hush man growled. "Now I suppose you'll say he's told you?"

"Well," said Ellery, "yes."

"Told you *what?*"

"Who the two foreign agents are."

Ellery explained to Storke: "Two of the facts you gave me were: first, that the foreign agents are listed in Monk's customer ledger; second, that each customer's name in the ledger is assigned an account number.

"Hartman made his extraordinary dying effort to call your attention to the otherwise empty can labeled MIX C. MIX C—two word-elements. And there are two agents. This could be a coincidence, but it could also mean that each of the word-elements identifies one of the agents.

"Pursuing this theory, I noticed something unusual about the letters composing the word MIX C that is not true about any of the phrases on the nine other labels on the shelf: *every letter in* MIX C *is also a Roman numeral.*

"You take MIX. M equals 1000; IX equals 10 minus 1, or 9. MIX therefore becomes the Roman numerology for 1009. I'm sure you will find, Storke, that the customer's name listed in the ledger microfilms opposite Number 1009 is that of one of the two foreign agents.

"C is simply the Roman numeral for 100, and I think you'll find Number 100 in the ledger is the name of the other agent."

Kidnaping Dept.:
The Broken T

Saturday 11:55 P.M.: Angie, not happily, turned into her street.

It was one of those dead-end streets on the far east side of midtown Manhattan made up of equal parts of warehouses, garages, renovated pre-1901 apartment buildings, and darkness. Lots of darkness.

Tonight the street wore a more sinister look than usual, which Angie blamed on the second feature she had just seen. The film, in explicit Spectracolor, had been a continuous horror of bile-green creatures pursuing a heroine of stainless steel nerve. How could any girl be so *brave?* Angie thought, cringing as she hurried into her unlit vestibule.

And screamed.

The scream came out a mumbly squawk, because a large spongy hand smelling of after-shave lotion and gun oil had leaped out of the dark and attached itself to her mouth. Two other hands—and that makes a pair of the beasts, the book-keeping division of Angie's brain recorded automatically—yanked her arms up behind her back and pushed.

"Whoa, bossie," gargled the pusher, still pushing. His breath sprayed sheer garlic.

"Hmmm gggnngle mmmffle," Angie said through the pain, offering to surrender the $9.63 in her purse. But it seemed that was not it at all. For Garlic Breath breathed, "You sure she's the Lawton broad?"; and a light exploded in her eyes and Lilac-and-Gun-Oil's voice replied, "Sure I'm sure. I studied her pitchers in the papers"; whereupon Garlic Breath said with chilling relish, "Then awayyyyy we go!"; and the light went out, leaving Angie in Spectracolor blindness and the horrid knowledge that this was no routine mugging after all.

The gears in her comptometer kept whirring as the pair dragged her out to a purring car, shoved her in headfirst, blindfolded her with something that smelled like a shoeshine rag, threw her on the car floor face down, and then one of them seated himself above her and dug his shoes into strategic sections of her anatomy as the other got behind the wheel and drove them away.

Angie knew now what it was all about. It had to have

100

something to do with the City Licensing Authority bribery scandal and the trial of the indicted Commissioner scheduled to begin on Monday morning.

She prayed briefly for the inhuman movie heroine's courage—which, being merely human, Angie knew she possessed in merely human quantity. But at the same time—for of such is the kingdom of bookkeepers—she found herself counting.

Sunday, 9:10 A.M.: How much of a beating did they give the girl?" Ellery asked Inspector Queen as they waited outside the hospital room for the district attorney to come out.

"Not enough to show and more than plenty to make their point," scowled his father. "A real pro workover, Ellery. Now she's too scared to testify. Maybe you can do something."

According to the Inspector's briefing, CLA clerk-typist-bookkeeper Angela Lawton, 23, blond, and pretty—upon whose testimony the City of New York was mainly relying for the conviction of the corrupt Commissioner—had been seized the night before by two men, driven blindfolded to an apartment somewhere, scientifically beaten, threatened with the destruction of her prettiness by acid if she testified on Monday, and dumped unconscious on her doorstep in the early hours of Sunday morning, where she was found by a prowl car.

The job had clearly been the work of musclemen in the defendant's behalf; but the girl had not once glimpsed the thugs' faces, and the chances of connecting the assault with the man going on trial seemed approximately zero.

"So there goes the D.A.'s case," said Inspector Queen, "unless we can get her to change her mind. Any luck, Herman?" he asked as the district attorney came out of the hospital room. The D.A. shook his head wanly and plodded away.

"Well, let's try ours," said Ellery, and they went in.

The girl was lying on the hospital bed like a stick.

"Now understand, Miss Lawton, nobody's blaming you one little bit," Ellery said tenderly, taking her hand. "A beating from professionals is a hard argument to top. But suppose we catch those men—make them talk, put them away. Then you'll have nothing to be afraid of, and you can testify. Right?"

The cold little hand tried to withdraw; tenderly, Ellery held on to it. "It's a big suppose, Mr. Queen. How are you going to catch them? I have no idea where they took me except that—"

"I know, you hurt all over," crooned Ellery as Angie stopped to wince. "Except that what?"

"—that wherever it is, it's across the street from a window with a neon sign in it. The blindfold slipped once while they were slamming me around, and before they could tighten it again I saw the sign flashing on and off in the dark. One neon sign—in the whole city of New York!"

"Pretty big odds," Inspector Queen said, showing his dentures in what he intended as a smile. "By the way, what did the sign say, Miss Lawton? Oh, and what color was it?"

"Pinkish-red. And the sign said EAT, in capital letters. How many of *those* do you suppose there are?"

"Hundreds, thousands," Ellery said. "Though neon signs do often become defective, Angie—you don't mind if I call you Angie? Did you happen to notice any imperfections in the letters?"

"There was a break in one of them," said Angie with a faint show of interest. "The T had an unlit gap, sort of. In the middle of the upright."

"E-A-broken T." Ellery beamed. "Across the street, you say. Oh, how about the drive over there? Did they drive fast?"

Angela's lip curled. "Think they'd take a chance on being stopped for a traffic violation? I paid particular attention to *that*. They didn't once exceed the speed limit. You can tell from the way it *feels*—at least, I can."

"I'll bet you can," said Ellery sincerely. "Though it's too bad you can't also tell us how long the drive took—"

"Oh, can't I," snapped Angie. "I know *exactly*. The moment the car started off I began to count in my head. At one-second intervals. I'm good at that—I practice with clocks for kicks. And of course I held up the count while it stopped for lights."

"Of course," Ellery said; his father was speechless. "Did you—er—stop to pay any tolls?"

"No. I didn't hear a single clink."

Ellery cleared his throat. "So you counted seconds. How many, Angie?"

"My count was 417 seconds for the trip. Allowing for error—say, seven minutes' riding time."

Ellery brought Angie's hand, which was quite warm by this time, to his lips reverently. "God bless your little bookkeeping head. There wouldn't be anything else, Angie, would there?"

Angie frowned. "Well, yes. They had my arms tied to the sides of a chair, but I managed to scratch an X on each side with my nails. But what good is that unless you find the room?"

In the corridor Ellery chortled, "What a girl! This ought to be peach pie, dad. Maximum average speed, say, thirty miles an hour—half a mile a minute. Time in motion, seven minutes. Maximum distance, therefore, three and one-half miles—"

"In any direction," his father pointed out dryly, "including circling back. Which means your three and a half miles could wind up in the next block."

"I'm talking maximums, dad. So that apartment has to be *within* three and a half miles of Angie's door. Figure twenty city blocks to the mile, and that's a radius of seventy blocks."

"In other words, anywhere between the East River and the Hudson east and west, and between—say—Houston Street and the Harlem River south and north." The Inspector sounded unimpressed. "And if your little lady's built-in computer happened to be off, it could be anywhere on Manhattan Island. That's a clue, that is."

"At least we know it's in Manhattan, dad—no tolls, Angie said. We also know the apartment faces a diner or cafeteria. And for that pink neon EAT sign to be visible through the apartment window, the apartment is almost certainly on a ground floor. Once we've found such an apartment, it can be positively identified by those X's Angie scratched on the chair. And that's it."

"You make it sound so simple," snorted the old man. "All right, Ellery, I'll put every available man on the streets to locate that diner or cafeteria. But you know what I think? I think this is a pipe dream!"

Sunday, 6:15 P.M.: The Inspector proved a prophet. As the last reports straggled in at headquarters, he said kindly, "Not a single diner or cafeteria in Manhattan with a broken-T EAT sign. So now what, my son?"

"Time," muttered Ellery, wearing a path in the Inspector's floor. "Time! The trial starts in less than sixteen hours . . . A neon sign with a broken letter—"

His father said, "What's the matter?"

"What's the matter?" screamed Ellery. "I'm an idiot is what's the matter! Not fit to carry that girl's penwiper! Dad, here's what you've got to do . . ."

Monday, 5:02 A.M.: So the Inspector did it; and here the Queens stood, on a nondescript Manhattan street in a

lightening hour, gazing on a plate-glass window behind which
a pinkish-red neon sign flashed on and off its 24-hour-a-day
message, EAT—with its T broken on the ascender exactly as
Angela Lawton had described it.

And following the possible lines of sight across the street,
Inspector Queen's men did indeed locate a ground-floor
apartment with a view of the EAT sign; and sleeping therein
they found a man with hands that smelled of lilac lotion and
gun oil, and they showed him the chair with the two
scratched-in X's, and the shoe rag with which Angie Lawton
had been blindfolded; and this bird was invited to raise his
voice in song, which after some encouragement he did, and
by 5:37 A.M. they had also flushed the other bird, Garlic
Breath, who was unmistakable.

They drove down to the hospital for a glad-happy-joyous
session with Angie; thence to the district attorney's office,
where the two birds sang a duet; and it all turned out fine,
except for the corrupt public servant.

Ellery had told Inspector Queen to have his men stop
looking for a diner or cafeteria and instead . . . But let Ellery tell it himself:

"Every eating place within the limits of the prescribed area
had been covered without turning up a neon sign such as
Angie described. Was it possible the sign *didn't* mean what it
seemed to say?—that the word was not EAT, but something
else?

"According to Angie, the sign had a defective T. Suppose
that was not the only defect in the sign? For instance, you're
always running across neon signs with entire letters blacked
out. Since it had been nighttime, Angie would only see the
letters that were lit up. Suppose EAT had a letter missing!

"The likeliest place for a missing letter in E-A-T is at the
beginning of the word. Run through the alphabet and you'll
find that only one letter, under the circumstances, makes
sense—M. So I suggested looking for a defective MEAT sign
in the window of a butcher shop, which is where they found
it."

Murder Dept.:
Half a Clue

Morning. When the doctor left, Ellery ran down to the corner drugstore.

"The doctor wants dad to start on the antibiotic as soon as possible, Henry," Ellery said to the owner of the pharmacy. "Can you fill this while I wait?"

"Sure, these come all made up," said Henry Brubuck. "Albert, fill this for Mr. Queen right away, will you?"

The twins, Albert and Alice, who like their stepfather were registered pharmacists, were busy behind the high partition of the Prescription Department. Albert took Inspector Queen's prescription and greeted Ellery heartily; but Alice, whose eyes were on the red side, merely gave him a wan smile.

"Sorry your father's sick, Ellery."

"It's some virus or other, Henry."

"The neighborhood's full of viruses. And that reminds me." The old pharmacist went over to his soda fountain and drew some water. "Forgot to take my own antibiotic dose this morning."

Henry Brubuck dipped into his gray store jacket for a little white box. It had some yellow-and-green capsules in it; he swallowed one and returned the box to his pocket. "Druggist, heal thyself, eh, Ellery?" he chuckled. "My doctor says I'm the worst patient he has."

"I live with an old coot, Henry, who'll give you cards and spades," said Ellery dolefully. "Thanks, Albert. Charge it, will you?" And he hurried out.

The moment Ellery was gone, Alice set a bottle of cough mixture down on the prescription counter and said tensely, "Dad, I've got to talk to you. *Please?*"

"All right, honey," sighed Henry Brubuck; he knew what was coming. "Take over, Albert. We won't be long."

"Good luck, sis," said Albert in a low voice. But his twin was already running up the stairs that led from the back room to the Brubuck apartment over the store.

Her stepfather followed patiently. A man did his best to bring up his dead wife's children, he thought, but somehow he always seemed to do the wrong thing. The twins were one problem after another; and he rarely saw his other stepson, Alvin, who was a used-car salesman, since Alvin's marriage.

"It's about Ernie again?" the old man asked his stepdaughter.

"Yes, daddy," said Alice passionately. "And please don't put me off any longer. I tell you I love Ernie. I want to marry him—"

"—but he won't marry you unless $10,000 goes along with you," her stepfather said dryly. "Some romantic! Honey, what kind of fellow is it who makes a package deal out of a marriage proposal? What kind of life would you have with a loafer who's even been in trouble with the police?"

Alice burst into heartbroken tears. "You think I'm Elizabeth Taylor or something? I know what I look like, daddy. If you don't give Ernie that money, he'll marry Sadie Rausch. I'll *die* if he does—I'll do something—something *desperate*."

Old Brubuck put his arm around the sobbing girl. "Don't talk like that, baby. Believe me, you're better off without him."

Alice raised her swollen eyes. "Then you won't give me the money? That's final?"

"It's for your own good, honey. You'll meet some nice boy—"

Alice grew very quiet. Then, just as quietly, she went back downstairs. Henry Brubuck stood where he was, appalled. There had been a look on his stepdaughter's face . . .

Noon. Old Brubuck was jarred out of his after-lunch nap by the eruption of the extension phone. Half asleep, he reached over from the bed and picked up the receiver just as the phone was answered in the Prescription Department downstairs.

"Brubuck's Pharmacy," he heard Albert say.

The old man was about to hang up when a heavy voice said, "Gimme Albert Brubuck. This is the book store."

Book store? thought Henry Brubuck, suddenly alert. Albert hadn't been inside a book store since leaving college. Had he been secretly playing the horses again? The pharmacist listened. He was right; it was Albert's bookie.

"Listen, welsher," the bookie said. "You think I'm gonna carry you forever? You're into me for eight grand, Pill Boy, and I want my dough. *Now*."

"Wait, wait," Albert said; his stepfather could tell that the boy was badly frightened. "So you'll have your goons work me over, Joe. How will that get you your money? Give me just another few days, Joe. What do you say?"

"Is this another one of your runarounds?"

"Joe, I swear, I'm working on the old man." Henry Brubuck could almost hear Albert sweat. "A few days more and I've got it made. How about it? All right, Joe?"

"Okay. But I don't get my eight grand by Friday night, kid, you start praying."

The pharmacist waited until his stepson hung up before replacing the bedroom receiver. So he's working on me, is he? thought the old man. Poor Albert. He wasn't a bad boy—except for the horses. Henry Brubuck had settled a great many of his younger stepson's gambling debts before putting his foot down; he had had to put a stop to it.

Then what had Albert meant . . . ?

Evening. The old pharmacist trudged upstairs from his drugstore and stopped in his kitchen to have a look at the roast that Alice had in the oven. He could hear his other stepson, Alvin, and Alvin's wife talking in the living room. Alvin had phoned with a rather ashamed, "Hiya, pop!" to invite himself and Gloria to dinner. The old man wondered what Alvin's wife was after this time.

He found out immediately—Gloria had a penetrating voice.

"Well, then you just ask that old miser *again,* Alvin! I'm not letting you pass up this chance to buy into the car agency for a measly $15,000!"

"But pop thinks they're in trouble and are out to take me," Alvin said feebly.

"Pop thinks! What does he know about it? Are you going back on your promise to me, Alvin Brubuck?"

"No, Gloria," said Alvin in a harassed way. "I told you I'd ask pop again, and I will. Do you have to keep hacking away at me?"

"And you remind him that most of the money he's got is really yours and the twins'. You *make* him give you your share, or else!"

"All right, all right!" shouted Henry Brubuck's other stepson. "I'll do whatever you want! Just stop hounding me!"

The Following Night. "I don't quite get what's bothering you, Henry," Inspector Queen said. He was in pajamas and bathrobe, still nursing his virus, but Ellery had long since given up trying to keep him in bed. "Okay, you won't buy Alice this crumbum the poor kid's set on marrying; you won't pay off any more of Albert's gambling debts—and don't worry about that bookie's threats, I'll take care of *him;*

you won't finance the partnership Alvin's wife wants because you're convinced it's a bad deal. Seems to me you're acting like a responsible parent. What's the problem?"

"The problem, I think, dad," said Ellery, frowning, "is that Henry is afraid for his life."

The Inspector stared. "You're kidding, Henry."

The pharmacist shook his head. "I wish I were, Inspector."

"But *murder?* All right, they're not your children. But the twins aren't delinquents, and no matter what a shrew Alvin's wife is, Alvin himself is a hard-working boy—"

"If you're right about this, Henry," Ellery said, "there's a simple way to discourage murder for profit. I take it you have a will, and that Alice, Albert, and Alvin get everything?"

"Of course."

"Then simply write a new will cutting them out. No profit, no danger, period."

Old Brubuck shook his head. "I can't do that, Ellery. I promised their mother on her deathbed that they'd inherit. Most of what I have she left me. Her children are entitled to it when I die."

"Drat it, Henry," the Inspector said testily, "if you're so sure they're out to kill you, give them the money now."

"I can't. It would bankrupt me. I'd even lose my drugstore." Brubuck laughed bitterly. "I'm losing my mind, too! I clean forgot to take my last dose of antibiotic. Ellery, could I have a little water?"

While Ellery went for some, the Inspector said, "Blast it all, Henry, I'm afraid there's nothing I can do *before* a crime is committed. That's the law."

"Besides which, Henry, you're holding something back," Ellery said as he returned with a glass of water. "I know you wouldn't dream up a murder plot merely on what you've told us. There's something more definite, isn't there?"

"I can't believe it yet," Brubuck nodded miserably. He fished a yellow-and-red capsule out of his little white box without even looking at it, and swallowed it with a sip of water. "But the fact is, some poison's been taken from a pharmaceutical cabinet in my back room."

The druggist named the poison, and the Queens exchanged grave glances; it was lethal in very small quantities, and it brought death on the gallop.

"I know it was stolen some time during the past thirty-six hours," Brubuck continued. "I even know which one of my stepchildren stole it, though I can't prove it."

"Why didn't you tell us this before?" the Inspector exploded. "Which one of them stole it?"

The pharmacist said with sudden difficulty, "It . . . was . . . Al—" and stopped with a gasp.

He began to choke and claw the air. An inhuman change came over his face. His body convulsed. His knees collapsed. Then, incredibly, he was spread out on the Queens' floor like a bludgeoned beef.

"*Dead.*" The Inspector, ghastly pale, looked up from the pharmacist's corpse. "Murdered in front of our eyes! Do you smell the poison, son?"

"It was in that capsule he just swallowed." Ellery snatched the white box from the quiet hand and opened it. It was empty. "It was his last dose, all right," he said wildly. "Why didn't I realize—?"

"Killed him as soon as the capsule dissolved." Inspector Queen was still dazed. "One of the three filled an empty capsule with the poison and managed to substitute it for the last antibiotic capsule in Henry's box. If he'd only lived long enough to finish the name . . ."

"Maybe," Ellery said suddenly, "it doesn't matter."

"But, son, all he got to say was 'Al—.' He could have meant Alice or Albert or Alvin. That's only half a clue—the useless half!"

"Half a clue, dad, is better than none."

The Inspector shot erect. "Ellery Queen, do you mean to stand here and say that Henry Brubuck drops dead at our feet, and practically as he hits the floor you know who killed him?"

Ellery said, "Yes."

Ellery explained that while he had been in the dead man's pharmacy the previous morning, waiting for the Inspector's prescription to be filled, he had witnessed Henry Brubuck take one of his own antibiotic capsules from the box —a yellow-and-*green* capsule.

"Just now," Ellery went on, "we both saw him swallow a yellow-and-*red* capsule from the box. Too bad Henry didn't bother to look at it—he knew there was only one left, or he'd certainly have noticed the discrepancy in color. And it all happened so fast I didn't have time to recall it.

"The question is, then: Which of Brubuck's stepchildren —he stated as a fact that he knew it was one of them—substituted a home-made yellow-and-red capsule containing poison for the last of the yellow-and-green manufactured capsules containing the antibiotic.

"Well, would a pharmacist, with a professional's knowledge of standard antibiotic preparations, have used *a different-colored capsule* when the object was to trick the victim, himself a pharmacist, into swallowing it? Hardly. Only a *non*-pharmacist could be guilty of such ignorance or oversight.

"So the poisoner can't be either of the twins, Al*ice* or Al*bert,* because both are registered pharmacists. Therefore it has to be the car salesman, Al*vin* . . . at the instigation, I'm afraid, of that virago he's married to."

Anonymous Letters Dept.:
Eve of the Wedding

The Mackenzie-Farnham nuptials—according to no less an authority than Violetta Billcox, Society Editor of the Wrightsville Record—were to be The Event of the summer social season. Molly Mackenzie was marrying Dr. Conklin Farnham, and nothing more important than that could be expected to happen for the rest of the year.

The bride-to-be was the daughter of the Donald Mackenzies (Wrightsville Personal Finance Corp., Country Club, Art Museum Committee, etc., etc.) and young Conk Farnham was *the* up-and-coming surgeon of Wrightsville—son of the celebrated New England internist, Dr. Farnham Farnham, who was President of the County Medical Association and Chairman of the Board of Wrightsville General Hospital. It was strictly a Skytop Road romance, for the Mackenzies' Virginia Colonial (built in 1946) was only two houses down the road from the Farnhams' redwood-and-glass Ranch-Type Modern; their back lawns embraced behind the skimpy acre of the Hallam Lucks' intervening estate.

It was to be a June wedding, of course, with the knot tied by the Bishop himself. The noted churchman was coming up from Boston especially for the ceremony, to the secret disappointment of Rev. Ernest Highmount, who had counted on the Mackenzies patronizing the local talent; in fact, Dr. Highmount had had Donald Mackenzie's half-promise to that effect. But Bea Mackenzie was as tough as the granite of the Mahoganies. Molly was her only child, and Bea had schemed and hoped for far too long to be deprived in her triumph of its full rewards. The Bishop it was going to be, with a lawn reception afterward for one hundred and fifty-six rigidly screened guests, and catering by Del Monica's of Connhaven.

"Connhaven! I'm in business in Wrightsville, Bea," protested Donald Mackenzie. "What's the matter with Liz Jones? Lizzie has catered every important shindig in this town for the last thirty-five years."

"Exactly," said Bea, patting her husband's paw. "How common can you get? Now you run along, Donald. All you have to do is pay the bills—I'll worry about everything else."

It was Bea who solved the social "problems." Conk was an absolute darling, but he *had* left rather a trail. There was Millie Burnett's Sandra, for instance—a large, panting girl with the disposition and intelligence of a healthy cow. Sandra was the outdoors type, and Conk had seen a great deal of her when he was wearing turtleneck sweaters—so much so that Sandra had grown stars in her eyes and Millie had bought her an outsized hope chest. Conk swore that he had never uttered a serious word to Sandra, the same being impossible; but to this day Millie Burnett spoke of him coldly.

There was also Flo Pettigrew, J.C.'s younger daughter, who had succeeded Sandra when Conk Farnham graduated from skiing parties on Bald Mountain to poetry sessions in the pines around Quetonokis Lake. Flo was pale and intense, wore her hair like the early pictures of Edna St. Vincent Millay, and was the Record's chief source of supply for love poetry; and when Conk broke their engagement she drooped like a bruised lily and wrote passionate verses to Death. Yet the Burnetts and the Pettigrews had to be invited to Molly's wedding; what was worse, Sandra and Flo were probably Molly's closest friends.

Bea solved the problem heroically: she convinced Molly that the course of wisdom was to pretend the past had never happened. Molly, who had inherited her mother's brains along with her father's good looks, had secret doubts; but she asked Sandra Burnett and Flo Pettigrew to be her bridesmaids anyway. When they accepted—Sandra with whoops and Flo very quietly—everyone was relieved but Conk Farnham.

Then Bea faced the question of what to do about Jen. Ordinarily a visiting relative from England would have given a fillip to a Wrightsville function; but Jennifer Reynolds, who was Bea's cousin and therefore her personal cross, drifted about the Mackenzie premises under such a pall of sorrow that she was bound to darken even so brilliant an occasion as Molly's wedding.

Bea gave a lot of thought to the problem of Jen. Finally

she announced, "What poor Jen needs in this crisis is a *man*."

"Oh, mother," said Molly. "I've thrown whole he-harems at her. Jen won't *encourage* an eligible male."

"Who?" sniffed her mother. "Dr. Flacker? Henry Granjon? All Walt Flacker knows about women is what he sees in the Maternity Pavilion. And Henry's idea of a jolly time is an evening of Canasta with his mother." Bea's snub nose wrinkled with cleverness. "The Lord knows, with Jen's mind she won't find a challenge in any man *Wrightsville* has to offer . . ."

"Who's the victim?" giggled Molly.

"Well," said her mother, not undefensively, "I *have* been trying to think up a formula for inviting Ellery Queen in from New York for the wedding . . ."

The last time Ellery had seen the principals, Molly had been a shy little bud at Wrightsville High and young Conklin Farnham a dedicated medical student apparently under the spell of one of the grimmer soap operas. Ellery found a full-grown radiant blossom and a hard-headed surgeon, and little opportunity to improve his acquaintanceship. For the Mackenzie house bustled with strange ladies with pins in their mouths, clanged with telephones and doorbells announcing the arrival of endless packages and cartons, and buzzed with mysterious conferences behind banged doors. Over all rose the conspiratorial laughter of Molly, Sandra Burnett, and Flo Pettigrew, occupied with whatever occupies the energies of a bride-to-be and her bridesmaids at such epic times. Occasionally Molly's groom flicked into the house in an aura of antiseptic, like a flung scalpel, bussed his bride in a dark corner, and flicked out again. Donald Mackenzie hardly showed his face; when he did, he was shooed off on some errand or other. As for Ellery's hostess, he met her at mealtimes only.

"We're neglecting you shamefully, Mr. Queen," Bea mourned, "but it's a comfort knowing we have Jennifer to entertain you. She's so much like you—quiet and deep, and interested in the arts and things. You'll find so much in common." And off she whisked, not neglecting to shut the door on them in her departure.

Jennifer Reynolds was a slight blond woman of thirty-four with a face whose charm looked as if it were regularly washed out in a strong bleach. It was chronically puckered, bothered by some mystery that defied solution.

There was a fragility about Mrs. Mackenzie's English cousin that made Ellery uneasy; and he was not surprised to learn that she was under the professional care of Conk Farnham's colleague, Dr. Walter Flacker, with whom young Farnham shared offices. But her fragility was more than physical. She was like a fine fabric worn to the nap and ready to fall to pieces at a touch.

One afternoon, when the bedlam was surpassing itself, Ellery drove Jennifer Reynolds up to the lake; and there, under the influence of the sun and the pines and the water peacefully lapping their drifting canoe, it all came out.

They were talking of Molly and her surgeon, and Ellery was saying what an ecstatically happy couple they seemed, and how sad it was that such bliss should be doomed to the usual corruption.

"Doomed? Corruption?" The Englishwoman looked up from her preoccupation with the ripples, startled.

"You know what I mean, Miss Reynolds. Marriages may be made in heaven, but how do they turn out?"

"Bachelor." She laughed, and lay back in the canoe. But then she sat up again, restlessly. "How wrong you are. They're very lucky, Molly and her Conklin. Do you believe in luck, Mr. Queen?"

"To a limited extent only."

"It's everything." Jennifer hugged her knees, and at the same moment a cloud slid before the sun and the air rapidly chilled. "Some of us are born lucky, and some of us are not. What happens to us in life has nothing to do with what we are, or how we're brought up, or what we try to make of our lives."

"The whole body of modern thought disagrees with you," Ellery smiled.

"Does it?" She stared at the riffling water. "I was working at a loom by the time I was fourteen. I never had the proper things, or enough to eat, or the means to make myself attractive. I didn't grouse; I tried very hard. I educated myself under great difficulties. I suppose Beatrice has told you that I write—criticism chiefly, and chiefly in the fine arts . . . During the war I fell in love. He was a Navy man. His ship was torpedoed in the North Sea and went down with all hands. We were to have been married on his next leave . . . I picked up the pieces of my life and carried on. I had my work, and I had my family, a very poor family, Mr. Queen, with an ailing father and mother and a great many younger sisters and brothers . . . all of us terribly devoted to one another. And then last February my entire family was wiped out in the floods that devastated the southeast coast of En-

gland. I was the only survivor; I was in London at the time.
So you see, I even had bad luck in that."

The bleached face puckered, and Ellery looked away and
said, "Well!" and picked up his paddle. "Rain clouds. Let's
get this relic of Hiawatha in, shall we, Miss Reynolds?"

He had to admit that Jennifer Reynolds had a case.

But there was less to be said for Sandra Burnett and Flo
Pettigrew. As the week jangled on, the sound of their laughter echoing Molly's took on the shrill pitch of hysteria. And
on the very night of the day Miss Reynolds gave him her
confidence, Ellery found out why.

Bea and Donald Mackenzie had gone down to High Village for a session with Avdo Birobatyan at the Wrightsville
Florist Shop, where a gardenia crisis had arisen. Conk and
Molly had driven off somewhere to be alone, Jennifer had retired early, Essie Hunker had washed the dishes and gone to
bed; and Ellery shut himself up in his room with some work
he had brought up from New York.

The house was quiet at last, and he became absorbed in
what he was doing. So when he heard the noise and glanced
at his watch, he was surprised to find that an hour had
passed.

The noise came from somewhere on the bedroom floor,
and Ellery opened his door and looked up the hall. Molly's
door was open and her light was on.

"Back so soon, Molly?" He paused in her doorway, smiling. She was standing in her wedding gown before the full-
length mirror in her dressing room, adjusting the bridal veil.
"Can't wait, I see."

And then she turned around and he saw that she wasn't
Molly Mackenzie at all, but Sandra Burnett.

"I beg your pardon," said Ellery.

Sandra's cheeks were gray under her tan. "I . . . just
stopped by," she said. "I thought nobody was home. I mean
—" And suddenly the big girl flopped onto Molly's vanity
bench and burst into tears.

"And not finding Molly here, you couldn't resist trying on
her wedding dress?"

"I'm so awfully ashamed," the girl sobbed. "But I always
thought Conk and I would . . . Oh, you don't understand!"
The gown was too small for her, and Ellery viewed its strain-
ing seams with alarm. "I'll never marry anyone else—never,
never . . ."

"Of course you will," said Ellery, "after you've found the
right man, who obviously isn't Conk. And we won't say any-

thing about this, Sandra, either of us. Now don't you think you'd better take that off—before Molly gets back?"

He heard the girl leave ten minutes later. The Burnetts lived only a short distance away; Sandra's flat heels pounded off down the road, as if she were running.

That was the first unusual incident of the evening. The second came much later, well after midnight. Bea and Donald Mackenzie had returned from the florist's in triumph and had gone to bed. It was a warm night, and Ellery went downstairs through the dark house and the open front door to the piazza, moving quietly. He sat down in one of the basket chairs, propped his feet on the porch railing, and soaked up the coolness.

He was still sitting there when Conk Farnham's convertible swung into the driveway and pulled up near the piazza. Ellery was about to announce himself when the motor died and the lights dimmed. He heard Molly's stifled laugh and Conk's manly, "Come here, you!" and decided that the immediate silence called for self-effacement. After a long moment Molly gasped, "No, darling, that's *all* for tonight—it's *late*," and Ellery heard her jump out of the car and run up the driveway to the side door.

And the moment the side door clicked shut on Molly, before Conk could turn on his ignition, there was a rustle of foliage from the rhododendron bushes on the far side of the driveway, and a woman's voice said, "Conk! Wait."

The young surgeon's surprised voice said, "Yes? Who's that?"

"Me."

"Flo! What are you doing here this time of night?"

"I've got to talk to you. I've been waiting behind that bush for hours. Let me get in, Conk. Drive me somewhere."

There was a pause. Then Conk said slowly, "No, Flo, I'd rather not. I've got to get home. I'm operating at eight in the morning."

"You've been avoiding me." Flo Pettigrew's voice sounded gurgly. "You're avoiding me now—"

"We have nothing to discuss," Ellery heard Conk say. "I broke our engagement because I realized we'd made a mistake. Would you rather I'd gone through with it, Flo, feeling the way I did? Anyway, that was kid stuff. Why revive it now? What can possibly be the point?"

"Because I still love you." Her voice was strangled.

"Flo, that's enough. This isn't fair to Molly." His voice was considerably sharper. "If you don't mind—"

"Oh, Conk, you never gave us a chance! We had so much

together . . . those firefly nights at the lake, our music, the poetry . . . Remember that Millay thing I told you was my own? 'I only know that summer sang in me/ A little while, that in me sings no more.' Oh, it was prophetic! I hate you!"

"Flo, you'll wake the house. Please take your hand off my car. I've got to get some sleep."

"You fool, you fool! Do you really believe that anyone as *childish* as Molly—?" The rest was smothered by the roar of the engine. The convertible backed rapidly out of the drive; in the glare of the headlights Ellery caught a glimpse of the thin pale face of Flo Pettigrew. Then the lights were gone, and Ellery clumped noisily into the house, rather hoping that the girl in the driveway could hear him.

The day before the wedding Molly had Sandra and Flo and five other girls in for brunch—"my last yak-party," Molly laughed. The yakking was vigorous—her father, home for lunch with Ellery on the side terrace, remarked that it sounded more like old man Hunker's barnyard at feeding time.

Molly insisted on dragging her friends out to the terrace to meet the author from New York, and Ellery spent a busy five minutes fending off the lion hunters and trying at the same time to read the faces of Flo Pettigrew and Sandra Burnett. But the poetess and the outdoor girl were quite unreadable. Both girls were a little pinched about the mouth, that was all. If anyone was nervous, it was the bride-to-be. Molly seemed tense and distracted in her vivacity. Ellery wondered if she had overheard the painful passage in the driveway the night before. And then he recalled that Molly had been nervous all the previous afternoon, too.

"Look at the time!" Molly cried. "Girls, you'll simply have to excuse us now. We're to meet Conk at the church—Dr. Highmount's running us through the rehearsal for the Bishop. Sandra, Flo, do the honors for me, will you, dears? Then come up and talk to me while I change. —And Daddy, don't forget, you're *not* to go back to the office. Mother said!"

Molly fled.

Sandra and Flo saw the girls to their cars while Ellery and his host finished their lunch. Essie Hunker was just serving the coffee when it happened.

Jennifer Reynolds appeared in the terrace doorway, pale as the tablecloth. "Donald, Molly's just had hysterics upstairs. I'm afraid she's fainted, too. You'd better come quickly."

"*Molly?*"

Molly's father ran, and Jennifer ran after him.

Ellery caught Molly's bridesmaids on the piazza, waving to the last departing car. He seized Sandra's arm. "Phone Conk Farnham—he's just up the road, isn't he? He must be home now, dressing for the rehearsal. Tell him to come right over. Something's wrong with Molly."

"Wrong!"

He caught one flash in Flo Pettigrew's eye, and then he ran back into the house and bounded upstairs. He heard Sandra excitedly jiggling the phone in the foyer as he reached Molly's bedroom.

Molly was lying in a heap on her dressing-room floor, her eyes closed, her cheeks chalky. Bea and Donald Mackenzie were on their knees trying to revive her. Bea was chafing the girl's left hand.

"Rub her other hand, Donald! Don't just squat there like a toad!"

"I can't get her fist open," groaned Molly's father. He began to massage Molly's right wrist. "Molly—baby—"

"Wake up, Molly!" Bea wailed. "Oh, dear, it's all this excitement today. I told her not to have those silly girls in—"

"Where's a doctor? Call a doctor!" Donald said.

Jennifer hurried in from the bathroom with a glass of water.

"He's already called," said Ellery cheerfully. "Here, let me get her onto the bed. You two parental idiots get out of the way. Mrs. Mackenzie, throw those windows wide open. Never mind the water, Miss Reynolds—she'd strangle. You hold her head way back while I lift. That's it . . ."

Ellery was still working unsuccessfully over Molly when Conk Farnham rushed in, his tie hanging unmade and lather still clinging to his cheeks.

"Out," he said hoarsely. "Everybody."

"But darling, *you?*" moaned Bea. "Conk, you *mustn't*—not the day before your *wedding*—"

He shut the door in her face.

Ten minutes later, Conk reappeared. "No, no, Bea, she's all right. She's out of it now. She's had some sort of shock—I can't get a thing out of her. What the deuce happened?"

"I don't know! Let me see my baby!" Bea said.

"Come in, but for heaven's sake don't excite her."

Molly was lying flat on her back in bed, covered to the chin and staring up at the ceiling. A little color had come into her cheeks, but her brown eyes were glassy with fear.

"Darling, what happened? What happened to my baby?"

"Nothing, Mother. Excitement, I suppose . . ."

Bea crooned over her.

"Donald," Conk said. "Do you have a sedative in the house?"

"Well, there's some sleeping pills in my medicine chest. Walt Flacker gave them to me for my insomnia a couple of weeks ago." He mentioned the brand.

"Even better. Warm a little milk and dissolve two tablets in it." Donald Mackenzie hurried out, and Conk went over to the bed and stroked Molly's bright hair. "I'm going to give you a soporific, young lady, and you're going to take it and like it."

"Oh, Conk, no," Molly whispered. "The rehearsal . . ."

"Hang the rehearsal. If you don't get some rest right now, there won't even be a wedding. Don't you want to be pronounced Mrs. Conklin Farnham tomorrow?"

"Don't say that!" Molly twisted into her pillow, sobbing.

Conk looked down at her, a crease between his eyes. Then he said pleasantly, "Bea, I think the caterer's people are downstairs waiting for you—I passed them on my way up. I'll stay with my patient till Donald brings up the milk. The rest of you—d'ye mind?"

Ellery was pacing the foyer when Donald Mackenzie came heavily downstairs again, followed by Jen Reynolds.

"How is she?"

"She drank the milk . . . I don't get it." Molly's father sank into the tapestried chair beside the foyer table.

"She still hasn't given an explanation?"

"No. There's something wrong, Mr. Queen—awfully wrong. But why won't Molly tell us?"

"There's nothing wrong, Donald," said the Englishwoman nervously. "Don't say things like that."

Ellery went to the front door and looked out. Bea Mackenzie was on the lawn talking to the caterer's decorators and glancing anxiously up at Molly's windows. Flo Pettigrew and Sandra Burnett were on the piazza, hands in their laps. He came back and said, "I disagree, Miss Reynolds. I think Mr. Mackenzie's right. Something caused that shock, and it wasn't just excitement."

"But Molly's one of the lucky ones!" cried Jennifer, as if Ellery had betrayed a sacred principle of hers.

Molly's father said between his teeth, "Something happened between the time she left the girls down here and the time she got to her room. You were upstairs, Jen. Did you hear or see anything?"

"All I know about it, Donald, is that I was in my room

when I heard Molly laughing and crying in the most peculiar way. I ran out and met Beatrice in the hall—she'd heard it, too. We ran in together and found Molly in her dressing room. She was having hysterics. Then her eyes rolled up and she fainted."

Donald Mackenzie looked at Ellery. "I don't like this at all," he said slowly. "Maybe I'm looking for trouble, but do you suppose, Mr. Queen, you could find out what's behind this?"

"Are you sure," asked Ellery, "that you want me to?"

"Yes," said Molly's father; and his jaw set.

Ellery turned to Jennifer Reynolds. "There was no one else in the room when you and Mrs. Mackenzie found Molly?"

"No, Mr. Queen."

"Nothing out of place? Lying on the floor?"

"I don't recall anything."

"Could she have had a phone call?"

"I heard no ring, Mr. Queen."

"I had one a few minutes ago," said Mackenzie. "But it's the only one I know of."

"Maybe a message of some kind. Did Molly get any mail this morning? A letter that perhaps she didn't open till she got upstairs?"

"Yes," said Molly's father suddenly. "When I got home for lunch I saw an envelope addressed to Molly lying in the tray here."

Ellery glanced at the salver on the foyer table. There was nothing on it. "Picked it up on her way upstairs. That may have been it, Mr. Mackenzie. Do you remember whom the letter was from?"

"I didn't look."

"What's this about a letter?" Conk Farnham came down the stairs, buttoning his collar.

Mackenzie told him. Conk shook his head. "I don't see how it can have been anything like that."

"How's Molly?" asked Jennifer.

"Corked off. She went out like a light." Conk went to the door and stared out at the two girls.

"I think," said Ellery, "we'd better look for the letter."

He found the envelope in the wastebasket in Molly's dressing room. It was lying on top of the heap, not even crumpled. And it was empty.

Ellery examined the envelope carefully, and his lean face lengthened.

"Well?" Donald Mackenzie licked his lips.

"All the earmarks of an anonymous letter," murmured Ellery. "Penciled address in block printing, dime-store envelope, and no return address. Postmarked yesterday. But where's the letter that came in it?"

Mackenzie watched dumbly as Ellery dumped out the contents of Molly's wastebasket and set to work. Halfway through, Ellery suddenly rose. "I just remembered. When we found Molly, one of her hands was so tightly closed you couldn't open it. I wonder . . ."

"I'll bet that's it!"

Mackenzie opened Molly's bedroom door softly. Conk had drawn the shades. They tiptoed over to the bed and peered down at the sleeping girl. Her right hand was still a fist.

"We mustn't wake her up," Mackenzie whispered.

Ellery stooped over Molly, his ear to her chest. He felt her forehead, touched her eyelids. Then he bolted to the door of the dressing room. "Conk!" he yelled. "Conk, *come back up —quick!*"

"But what's the matter now?" faltered Mackenzie.

Ellery brushed by him, returning swiftly to the girl's bedside. Footsteps rattled in the hall. Conk Farnham burst in, the girls and Bea at his heels.

"What is it?" Conk asked wildly.

"There's something wrong with her breathing and heart action," Ellery said.

After a frantic examination Conk glared at his prospective father-in-law. "What the devil did you put in that milk?"

"Only two of the sleeping pills," stammered Molly's father.

"She's had a heavy overdose of the drug! Bea, Jen—I'll need both of you for a while. The rest of you get out!"

"But I only did what you told me," Donald Mackenzie moaned.

Ellery had to remove him forcibly.

"Listen to me, Mr. Mackenzie!" In the hall Ellery backed the bewildered man against the wall. "You're in for a shock —the same shock that made Molly faint." He produced a small wrinkled sheet of cheap white paper. "I took this out of Molly's fist."

The Wrightsville businessman stared at the writing on the paper. Nine words, in the same penciled block printing of the envelope:

"You ignored my warning, so you will die today."

If not for Jen, as Bea said afterward, they would all have gone to pieces then. Jen was a tower of strength, managing to be everywhere at once—soothing Bea, assisting Conk, slapping Sandra when the big girl began to heehaw like a hysterical mule, getting Flo's ill-timed storm of tears under control, and coming down hard on Essie Hunker, who sat in the kitchen with her apron over her head shrieking like a banshee.

"I was born to trouble," said Jen with a sort of pride; and she carried on.

Ellery asked questions and prowled. It was he who brought down word from Conk that Molly was conscious and out of danger; she was sick and still dazed, but she would be all right. Conk forbade anyone to come upstairs until he called.

They sat huddled in the living room, and from the lawns came the cheery sounds of the caterer's people stringing Japanese lanterns, sparkly mobiles, and ropes of evergreens.

"As long as we have to wait," remarked Ellery, "we may as well employ the time gainfully. Let's see if we have the facts straight.

"When Conk told you to prepare the sleeping draught, Mr. Mackenzie, you took your bottle of pills down to the kitchen and set some milk to heat on the range. You opened the bottle and were about to take two tablets out when Essie called you to the phone. The minister was asking about the rehearsal. You took the call in your library, leaving everything in the kitchen as it was. Essie, who was cleaning up the dining room and terrace, was out of the kitchen all the time you were telling Dr. Highmount about Molly's fainting spell. Then you came back, turned off the range, dropped two tablets into the milk, dissolved them, poured the contents into a glass, and took the glass upstairs. You stood there while Conk put the glass to Molly's lips and she drank the milk. And within a short time, Molly was drugged.

"It's obvious, then," said Ellery in the silence, "that someone who had planned it perhaps a different way saw a better opportunity when you left the kitchen to answer the phone, and took advantage of your absence to slip into the kitchen and dose the milk heavily from the bottle on the table. When you returned, you merely added two more pills."

"My fault," said Molly's father dully. "I didn't notice that the bottle, which had been almost full, was half empty when I got back. I was so upset about Molly——"

Bea pressed her husband's hand. But her eyes remained on Sandra Burnett and Flo Pettigrew, and there was a lethal glitter in them.

"The point is," said Ellery, "someone here tried to murder Molly, and it could have been anyone in the house."

And there was another silence.

"Are you looking at me?" screamed Flo Pettigrew. "Do you think I'd do a thing like that?"

"Yes," said Bea Mackenzie.

"Beatrice," cried Jennifer.

Flo sank back, trembling. And Sandra Burnett sat there with a witless look on her face, as if she could not understand any of this.

"I still can't believe it," muttered Mackenzie. "That one of Molly's girl-friends . . ."

"Murder is always hard to believe, Mr. Mackenzie."

"The police—the wedding . . . It's all spoiled now."

"Not necessarily. There's no reason to call Chief Dakin yet. By the way, I've made another discovery."

"What now?" It brought all their heads up.

"The letter indicated a *previous* warning. People embarking on a spree of crime usually establish a pattern of behavior. So I looked for another anonymous note; and I found it in one of Molly's coats—the coat she was wearing day before yesterday."

"Give—me—that!" grated Donald Mackenzie.

The sheet of paper was identical with the one they had found in Molly's hand. There was no envelope. The message was block printed, in pencil. Mackenzie read it aloud slowly.

"Call off your wedding to your fine Mr. Farnham, or you'll be very sorry. Remember Browning's Laboratory."

"That's why she was nervous yesterday," exclaimed Jen. "The poor, poor dear."

"Browning's Laboratory!" Molly's father looked up at Ellery, frowning. "What's that mean?"

"I don't know. I was hoping you could tell me."

"Browning's Laboratory . . ." He turned to his wife. "Do we know anybody named Browning?"

"No, Donald." Bea was scarcely listening; her eyes were still on Molly's bridesmaids, and they still glittered.

"How about Molly?" asked Ellery. "Perhaps a high school teacher—chemistry lab, that sort of thing. Do you girls know?" he said suddenly, turning to Sandra and Flo.

They shrank. "No," said Sandra. "No!"

Flo Pettigrew shook her head violently. She was very pale.

"I don't think there's a single family in Wrightsville by that name," rasped Mackenzie. "There's a Brownell Dental Laboratory in Limpscot, but that can't . . ."

"All right now!" Conk Farnham's voice from upstairs rang through the house like a jubilee gong.

The rush left Ellery alone in the living room. He sank into

a chair, staring at the note. He sat there for a long time. Then he got up and made for the Mackenzies' library.

"Well, we're *not* going to call off our wedding," Conk Farnham was announcing when Ellery walked into Molly's bedroom. "Are we, honey?"

Molly smiled faintly up at him. "Not a chance." Her voice was low but clear. "I'm not scared any more."

"We'll be married tomorrow on schedule, and no murdering sneak is going to stop us." Conk glared at the two girls cowering near the windows.

"May I—may we go home now?" Flo sounded far away.

"P-please . . ." blubbered Sandra.

"No!" roared Conk. "Because now— Oh, Ellery. What do you make of this 'Browning's Laboratory' business? Seems to me there's a clue there."

"Definitely," smiled Ellery. "Well, Molly. You look human again."

"Thanks, Mr. Queen," whispered Molly, "for catching me in time . . ."

"Rescuing brides for their grooms is my specialty. Oh, by the way," Ellery held up a fat green book he was carrying. "Here's the answer to that cryptic reference."

Bea Mackenzie stared. "That's my volume of Robert Browning's poetry that all us girls get when we join the Robert Browning Society. Did it mean *my* Browning, Mr. Queen?"

"Your Browning," nodded Ellery, "and his Laboratory. 'The Laboratory' is the title of one of Browning's poems. Since the writer of the note wanted Molly to 'remember' this particular poem, let me tell you what it's about." He looked around benignly. "It's about a woman who, discovering that the man she loves is in love with another woman, procures some poison to kill her successful rival. That's the plot line . . . Those notes were a warning, all right—a warning from a woman who thinks she's in love with Conk, and who's tried to kill you, Molly, to prevent your marrying him. Sheer envy, grown to homicidal proportions. Shall I tell you," said Ellery, "which woman it was?"

"Wait!" Molly bounced upright. "Wait, Mr. Queen, please! Were you—were you going to give me a wedding present?"

Ellery laughed and took Molly's cold little hand in both of his. "Some such thought had crossed my mind. Why, Molly?"

"Because there's only one present I want," cried Molly. *"Don't tell who it was.* Please?"

Ellery looked down at her for a long time. Then he squeezed her hand. "You're the doctor's wife," he said.

It was very late. The moon had set; the lawns were black behind the night breeze. There were no lights in the windows; everyone was asleep, exhausted by the events of the day. Up the road the Farnham house was dark, too.

"I think you know what I have to say," Ellery was murmuring to the silent figure in the other lawn chair, "but I'm going to say it anyway.

"You won't get another opportunity to harm Molly—I'll see to that. And since Molly wants this kept quiet, I suggest you'd better find an excuse for leaving Wrightsville immediately after the wedding tomorrow. In fact, we can arrange to go together. How would you like that?"

There was no sound from the other chair.

"People who do what you did are ill. Suppose I send you to someone in New York who's very good at straightening out sick minds. You'll have your chance, and I strongly advise you to take it."

The figures rustled, and a wraith of a voice drifted over through the darkness. "How did you know?" it said.

"Well, it goes back quite a way," said Ellery. "To the Middle Ages. Even earlier, in fact, to the Fifth Century A.D. and the barbers of Rome."

"Barbers?" said the voice, bewildered.

"Yes. Because barbers were the only people until relatively recent times who practiced surgery. It wasn't till shortly before the American Revolution that the barbers and surgeons of London, for instance, were split into two separate groups, and in France, Germany, and other European countries the practice of surgery by barbers wasn't forbidden by law until much later.

"So to be a surgeon, you see, was for centuries considered a lowly occupation. So lowly, in fact, that surgeons weren't dignified by titles. And the prejudice has carried over into modern times in some countries. To this day the most eminent surgeons of the finest British hospitals are not addressed as 'Doctor,' like other medical practitioners, but as 'Mister.'

"And so," said Ellery, "when I thought over the note that referred to Dr. Conklin Farnham, a surgeon, as *'your fine Mr. Farnham,'* I realized that only one person in the house —in all of Wrightsville, for that matter—could have written it, and that was the visiting gentlewoman from England. You, Miss Reynolds."

Probate Dept.:
Last Man to Die

For well over once around the clock Ellery tried to breathe life into The Butler who was lying in the way of the new Queen novel's progress.

In the fourteenth futile hour Ellery detected the difficulty: it was so long since he had seen a real live butler that it was like trying to bring a brontosaurus to life.

The situation obviously called for research; and making a haggard mental note to start looking for a specimen—assuming the breed was not extinct—Ellery collapsed.

He had no sooner closed his eyes, it seemed, than the alarm clock brought him up with a leap, groping. Noting blearily that the time was 8:07 A.M. and the alarm was off, he concluded: It's the doorbell ringing. And he staggered to the apartment door to find himself blinking out at a girl, 38-23-36, with eyes of blue, and red hair, too. Oh, brother!

"Mr. Queen?" asked a voice like temple bells, eying the Queen dishevelment doubtfully. "Am I inconvenient?"

"Not even after only two hours and eleven minutes' sleep," said Mr. Queen, quickly showing her in. "With whom do I have the pleasure?"

"Edie Burroughs," said the belle with the bell voice, turning pink and pleased, "and I have a problem."

"Haven't we all? Mine concerns a butler."

"Well, isn't that weird!" she cried. "So does mine. In fact, two of them. Did you ever hear of The Butlers Club?"

"May we make haste slowly, Miss Burroughs?" begged Ellery, dragging over a chair. "*Two* butlers? The Butlers *Club?* Where? When? In short, what?"

The goddess graciously explained. Aphrodite-like, The Butlers Club had risen out of the golden foam of the '20s. Hoity-toitier than even the Union, Century, or Metropole clubs, its membership had been restricted to the thirty noblest butlers of them all, who pooled their considerable resources and leased a haughty brownstone in the Sixties, just off Fifth Avenue, for their clubrooms.

By 1939 the depression and natural causes had lopped the membership to a butler's dozen. But the club treasury took on a hideous life of its own, for the survivors—privy to the financial secrets of their multimillionaire employers—invested in common stocks for $5 and less a share, and by 1963 the club owned the brownstone and $3,000,000 worth of blue-chip securities besides.

Today a mere two members, long since retired from butling, survived. Both were in their 80s—William Jarvis (who had, it appeared, a repulsive grandson named Benzell Jarvis), and Peter Burroughs, Edie's grandfather, both of who lived at the club.

"Ben Jarvis and I lead lives of our own elsewhere and," Miss Burroughs added grimly, "apart, thank goodness. But under the bylaws the members must live at the club or forfeit their rights of survivorship."

"Rights of *survivorship?*" Mr. Q was sniffing like an enchanted hound dog. "Do you mean to say this association of majordomos created a tontine? That wonderful old stupidity in which everything goes to the last beneficiary left alive?"

"Yes, Mr. Queen."

"I'm amazed. Butlers are supposed to be the most conservative group on earth."

"You evidently don't know much about butlers," chimed Miss Burroughs. "They're all born gamblers. Anyway, by now those two old ninnies have only one thought—to outlive the other and so fall heir to the club treasury. It's all pretty silly, and it would be amusing if not for the fact . . ." She hesitated.

"If not for what fact?"

"Well, that's really why I'm here, Mr. Queen. Last evening I dropped by for my weekly visit to grandfather . . ."

The Night Before, 7 P.M.: Edie found the pair of octogenarians in the oak-and-leather "silence room," engaged in making a great deal of what, in any but butlers, would have been unseemly noise.

"And you, Jarvis," Edie heard her grandfather shout in an undertone, "have a narsty mind!" Peter Burroughs was a long withered root of a man, all crooked with age, and he was vibrating as in a high wind.

"Really, Burroughs?" chortled William Jarvis. Jarvis was little and bald and livid, and the chortle sounded remarkably evil. "Can you deny trying to put me out of the way in order to be able to leave the club fortune to your granddaughter?"

"I can, Jarvis, and I do!"

"*Mr.* Jarvis, really," said Edie, shocked. "Nobody's trying to put you out of the way."

"No, indeed, you doddering scullion," said old Burroughs to old Jarvis in a refined shriek. "The boot is quite on the other foot! It is *you* who are planning to kill *me* for the tontine, to pass it over to that playboy grandson of yours!"

And the two old men tottered toward each other's throats, claws at the ready.

At that moment, fortunately, Benzell Jarvis arrived on *his* weekly visit, which always seemed to coincide with Edie's, and stepped between the bristling gaffers. For once Edie was glad to see him (young Jarvis, who was an exemplary Dr. Jekyll in company, became an instant Mr. Hyde when he could catch Edie alone).

"Here, Edie," said Ben Jarvis, who was as little and bald as his grandfather, "you take your old fool, and I'll take my old fool, and we'll put 'em away—I wish there were locks on their bedroom doors—and then . . . you and me . . . ?"

". . . but I'm worried half to death, Mr. Queen," Edie concluded, not mentioning the judo chop she had had to resort to in escaping from young Mr. Jarvis. "Each thinks the other is out to murder him, and they might do each other real harm in imagined self-defense. It seems ridiculous to go to the police, and yet—what shall I do?"

"Don't they employ anyone to take care of them?"

"The houseman and the cook work afternoons only; they sleep out. Nobody's there at night if one of them should get a senile notion."

"Then what is required in this emergency," said Ellery with gravity, "is an unofficial show of authority. My father is a police inspector, Miss Burroughs, and this is just the kind of crime-prevention work he dotes on. Excuse me while I telephone him."

Later: For a man who doted on crime prevention, Inspector Queen seemed extraordinarily unenamored of this particular opportunity. The Inspector glared at his son as they waited with Edie Burroughs on the sidewalk in front of The Butlers Club for Ben Jarvis (the Inspector had insisted on phoning him to join them); he glowered at Jarvis as that young man, clearly suffering from hangover, crawled out of a cab; and as they all mounted the brownstone steps he muttered to Ellery, "What in the so-and-so is the goldang idea?"

But he pressed the bell. And again. And again, and again. "Are they deaf as well as mush-headed?" the Inspector growled.

"It's a very loud bell," said Edie Burroughs nervously. "Oh, do you suppose—?"

"Allow me," said Ellery, whipping out his trusty picklock

gun. He unlocked the door and they stepped through a time machine into a living past of dark woods, altitudinous ceilings, vast stained-glass chandeliers, brassy firedogs, and many many oil paintings of—incredibly—butlers.

And, oddly, a continuous trilling sound.

"That's grandfather's alarm clock," Edie exclaimed, "in his bedroom. Why doesn't he turn it off?"

She bounded like Artemis toward the rear of the main floor, explaining on the fly that her grandfather could no longer climb stairs. And as she burst into the old butler's bedroom the girl wailed, and stopped, and turned away; and just as the Queens sprang to the big brass bed to stoop over Peter Burroughs, the old-fashioned single-alarm clock on the nightstand uttered a last peevish screek and went as dead as its owner.

Old Burroughs, fully dressed, was sprawled across the bed. There were several ugly scratches on his barklike cheeks, but no other signs of violence.

"From the condition of the body, he's been dead since last night," said Inspector Queen after a while. "Did he have those face scratches when you two left here?"

"No," said Ben Jarvis, absently embracing Edie. "Tough luck, sugar. My condolences."

"Thank you, Ben," said Edie, "but no hands? Please?"

"I think, Jarvis," said Ellery, eying Ben coldly, "we had better look in on your grandfather, too. Where is his bedroom? Upstairs? No, Miss Burroughs, you'd better wait for us down here."

So they found little old William Jarvis crumpled on his bedroom floor, fully clothed also; and *his* cheeks were badly scratched; and he was just as dead as his fellow butler below.

"When," asked young Jarvis wildly, "did *he* die?"

And the Inspector rose and said, "Last night, too."

"At 7:46," Ellery nodded, pointing to the bedside electric clock. In falling, the old man's body had jerked the cord out of the wall socket, stopping the clock. "What time did you and Miss Burroughs leave here last night, Jarvis?"

"Not quite 7:30."

They found Edie in the big clubroom downstairs, weeping quietly. She looked up and said, "Dear God, what happened?"

"I'd say they waited until you two left," Inspector Queen said, "and then headed for each other again. The only damage they were able to do was scratch each other's faces, but the exertion and excitement must have been too much for both of them. They managed to get back to their bedrooms, collapsed, and died. I'm betting the postmortems show simple heart failure in both cases."

"There, there," Ellery was crooning to the flooded blue eyes. "They were very old, Edie."

"Thus endeth The Butlers Club, and high time, too," said Benzell Jarvis. "All I want to know is, which one died first? Or rather, second?"

"No autopsy can determine the exact moment of death," the Inspector said, regarding him as if he were a strange bug, "although I'm positive they died around the same time. You know, Ellery, it makes an interesting problem at that."

"What, dad?" said Ellery. "Oh! Yes. It does, indeed."

"You're damned right it does!" snarled Jarvis. "If old Burroughs died first, my grandfather inherited the tontine and I get the jackpot. If it was the other way around, Edie gets it. There's got to be some way of telling which survived the other, even if it was only for ten seconds!"

"Oh," said Ellery, "there is, Jarvis, there is."

As Ellery explained it: "We know what time William Jarvis fell dead last night. The electric clock he stopped in falling says it was 7:46.

"The question, then, is how to determine what time Peter Burroughs died. His alarm clock provides the answer.

"If you want an alarm clock to ring at, say, 8 o'clock in the morning, you must set the alarm *after* 8 o'clock the night before. Because if you set the alarm before 8, it will obviously ring at 8 the same night, not at 8 the next morning.

"It was a few minutes past 8 A.M. when Edie Burroughs came to me for help this morning. I had to call you, dad; you called Ben Jarvis; we all had to meet on 60th Street—it was therefore long past 8 A.M. when we entered The Butlers Club. And what did we hear when we entered? The ringing of Peter Burroughs's alarm clock, which ran down just as we got into his bedroom.

"Therefore Peter Burroughs must have set his alarm long past 8 o'clock last night. To have been able to do that, he had to have been alive long past 8 P.M.

"But your grandfather, Jarvis, died at 7:46 P.M.

"Miss Burroughs, may I shake the hand of the loveliest multimillionaire of my acquaintance?"

Crime Syndicate
Dept.: Payoff

"Combine?" Ellery asked, sitting up.

"No," sighed Inspector Queen, "these operators are about as close to the Combine type as the stratosphere to a ground-hog. And as hard to reach. It's a real high-class nastiness."

"Tell me more, dad."

"Well, we were up against a stone wall till evidence turned up that this plush-lined mob has a Board of Directors composed of four men. When I tell you who they are you'll send for the loony wagon."

"It can't be as bad as all that."

"Can't it?" The Inspector raised his corded hands and began to tick the quartet off. "One: Ever hear of DeWitt Hughes?"

"Certainly I've heard of DeWitt Hughes. Wall Street and banking in the megamillions. You're not seriously suggesting . . . ?"

"I am."

"But DeWitt Hughes? Directing a crime syndicate?"

"As one of four," said his father, shaking his head. "Of whom the second is John T. Ewing."

Ellery gawped. "The oil and mining tycoon?"

"You heard me. And Number Three: Filippo Falcone."

"The construction and trucking king? Dad, is this a rib?"

"I wish I could joke about it," the Inspector said. "And last —you ready, son? Reilly Burke."

"You've got to be kidding," Ellery exclaimed. "Burke, the Great Mouthpiece of our time! Why would a lawyer of Burke's standing and big businessmen like Falcone, Ewing, and Hughes dirty themselves in the rackets?"

The old man shrugged. "Maybe it's so easy for such operators to make big money legit these days that the only kicks left is to turn crooked."

"I'd like to help straighten them out," Ellery said grimly. "I take it I fit into your plans some way?"

"Before we move a step I want to know which of those four cuties is top banana, Ellery. Not only would that enable us to move in faster and so cut down on the chances of a tipoff, but my information is that the head man has possession of the main syndicate records. So I'm hoping you can pinpoint him for us."

"Do you have a lead?"

"In a way." Inspector Queen flipped his intercom. "Velie, send in Mrs. Prince."

The ravaged woman Sergeant Velie admitted to the Inspector's office must once have been pretty in a petite, even chic, way. But only wreckage was left. She was so nervous that Ellery had to help her into the chair; her arm thrummed like a piano wire.

"Mrs. Prince's husband is an accountant who's serving five to ten for an embezzlement," Inspector Queen said.

"He didn't do it." She had a broken-down voice, too. "He confessed to a crime he didn't commit because it was part of a deal."

"Tell my son what Mr. Prince told you when he was sent up."

"John said that when he got out we'd be set for life," the woman told Ellery. "Meanwhile, every month for over three years now I've received through the mail an unmarked envelope containing $750 in small bills. That's what the children and I have been living on."

"You don't know where the money is coming from?"

"No, and John won't discuss it when I visit him. But he knows, all right! It's part of the deal he made, I'm positive, to make sure he keeps his mouth shut."

"He's being released from Sing Sing on parole tomorrow, Ellery."

"My husband told me not to meet him in Ossining—to wait for him at home," the woman whispered. "Mr. Queen, I'm scared."

"Why?"

"Because of the deal he made, whatever it was. Of the blood money, wherever it comes from, that he's going to be paid off with. I don't want it!" Mrs. Prince cried. "All I want is for us to get away from here, change our name, start all over again somewhere. But John won't listen to me . . ."

"Or to anyone else," said Inspector Queen. "It's a long shot, Ellery, but maybe he'll listen to you. Mrs. Prince says he's always been a fan of yours."

"If you'd only make John see that we can't build a life on that kind of money, Mr. Queen!"

"Nobody, including you, is going to talk Prince out of *that*," the Inspector remarked to his son, when the woman had left, "in spite of what I just said. Not when he's earned the money by sacrificing his good name and over three years of his life."

"Then what's the point, dad? And what does it have to do with the crime syndicate you're investigating?"

"We've found out," his father answered, "that before Prince was sent up he handled a lot of highly confidential work for Hughes, Ewing, Burke, and Falcone; in fact, the embezzlement rap stemmed from a job he did for one of Hughes's banks. He's denied it, but I have good reason to believe Prince was close to the big boys and knows who the head man is. Maybe you can think of a way to trick the information out of him."

"And he's coming home tomorrow?" Ellery looked thoughtful. "All right, dad. Let's form a reception committee."

At 2:15 P.M. the following day the reception committee turned out to have a noisy, and unexpected, counterpart.

The Inspector's men were routinely staked out in various vestibules and tradesmen's entrances in the vicinity of the modest East Side corner apartment building in which the Princes lived. A taxi turned into the street and pulled up before the building. John Prince got out. The cab drove off, and the emaciated, rather stooped figure of the accountant turned toward the building.

At that instant a nondescript black sedan with muddied license plates careened around the corner and began to chatter and spit fire as it bolted past Prince and up the street and around the corner. Prince fell to the sidewalk, staining it red as he hit.

Squad cars roared futilely off after the vanished murder car as the Queens and Sergeant Velie ran over to the quiet man. They were almost, not quite, too late.

Sergeant Velie took one look and advised, "Better step on it."

"Prince. Prince, listen," Ellery said, stooping over him. "Help us get them. Talk. Can you talk?"

"Four . . . of them," gasped the dying man, looking into Ellery's eyes. "Each one uses . . . a code name . . . of a city."

"Four cities?"

"Boston . . . Philadelphia . . . Berkeley . . ." The voice guttered like a burned-out candle. Prince made one incredible effort. "And Houston," he said, quite clearly.

"Which one is top man?"

But the accountant's stare glassed over and remained that way.

"Bye-bye, blackbird," announced Sergeant Velie.

"So my hunch was right," muttered Inspector Queen. "He did know. One second—one second more!—and he'd have told us. No, Velie, let her," he said in a gentler tone. "Mrs. Prince, I'm sorry . . ." The old man sounded sorry for a number of things.

The widow stood over her husband's body. "Now you know, John," she said to it. "Now you know how they meant to set you up." And she brushed by the Inspector's proffered arm and went blindly back into the apartment building.

"Well?" the Inspector snapped to his son after a while. "Don't stand there with your mouth hanging open! This code business ought to be your candy; each of the four using the name of a city for identification! What did he say they were again?"

"Boston, Philadelphia, Berkeley, Houston." Ellery was still returning the dead man's stare. Then he turned aside and said, "For the love of heaven, Velie, close his eyes, will you?"

"Well, it doesn't matter. We knew who they are," and the Inspector turned away, too. "The only thing we didn't know —the name of the head man—he didn't get to tell us."

"Oh," said Ellery, "but he did."

Ellery's solution: "If you examine them, there's a connection between the names of the crime directorate and the city code names they chose to cover their identities.

"Take one: Reilly *Burke* and the city of *Berk*eley. Burke —Berk. Identical in sound.

"Or take *Fi*lippo Falcone and *Phil*adelphia. Fil—Phil."

"Oh, come on, Ellery," said Inspector Queen. "Coincidence."

"Then how about DeWitt *Hughes* and *Hous*ton? Hughes —Hous. Two might be a coincidence. Three? No, sir."

"But that leaves John T. Ewing and the code name of Boston. Find me a connection between those two!"

"Ah, that's the missing ingredient," Ellery said, watching the meat wagoneers trundling their poor freight away. "In each city name the corresponding clue was in the first syllable: Berk, Phil, Hous. Try it on Boston."

"Boston. Bos." The Inspector looked doubtful. Then he cried. *"Boss!"*

"Ewing is obviously the head man you're trying to identify," Ellery nodded. "The Boss."

THE PUZZLE CLUB

The Little Spy

The letter was written in a secretive hand on paper as thick as a pharaoh's papyrus. Instead of a name or a crest, its engraved monogram consisted of one large, gold, ticklesome question mark.

"My dear Mr. Queen," Ellery read. "It is the pleasure of The Puzzle Club to invite you to our next regular meeting, which takes place at 7:30 P.M. Wednesday at the address below. Purpose: to offer you our membership test, which we believe without modesty will challenge your logical powers.

"Ours is a very small, congenial group. There are no dues or other obligations. You will be the only outsider present. Informal dress.

"We hope you will respond affirmatively."

None of Ellery's reference books, including the telephone directory, listed a Puzzle Club. On the other hand, the signature and address made it unlikely that this was the gambit to a mugging party or badger game. So Ellery dashed off an acceptance note; and Wednesday evening found him, at 7:30 to the tick, pushing the bell of a penthouse foyer in the nobbiest reaches of Park Avenue.

The lordly Englishman who opened the door turned out to be a butler, who took his hat and vanished; and the rumpled-looking Texan giant who greeted him was unmistakably Ellery's correspondent and host. The big man's name was Syres, and he was one of the ten wealthiest men in the United States.

"On the dot," Syres boomed. "Welcome, Mr. Queen!" He was all but grinding his muscular hands; and he rushed Ellery

into a museum of massive Western furniture, studded leather,
burnished woods, antique carpets, old masters, and twinkling
crystal and copper. "I see you're admiring my traditionalism.
I loathe contemporary anything." Except, Ellery thought,
contemporary oil wells and the profits therefrom; but he
meekly followed his host into a living room vast enough for a
hidalgo's rancho.

In a moment Ellery was shaking hands with the other
members of The Puzzle Club. Three were present besides
Syres, and not altogether to his surprise Ellery recognized
each of them. The dark, tall, mustache-eyebrowed man was
the celebrated criminal lawyer, Darnell, who was being mentioned frequently these days for the next opening on the Supreme Court. The trim, short, peach-cheeked one was the
noted psychiatrist, Dr. Vreeland. The third was Emmy Wandermere, the poet, a wisp of a woman with shocking blue
eyes and the handclasp of a man.

Ellery gathered that The Puzzle Club was of recent origin.
It had no more purpose than any other association in games-
manship, perhaps less; and while its members were all promi-
nently implicated in the world as it was, the Club's bylaws, he
was promptly told, forbade discussion at its monthly meetings
of any subject not connected with puzzles. As the psychiatric
Dr. Vreeland put it, "Other people meet regularly to play
bridge. We meet to mystify each other—as man has done
with riddles since prehistory—in a sort of ritual adoration
of the question mark."

They sat him down in a roomy armchair near the man-
high fireplace, and the English butler brought him a Scotch, a
napkin, and a little tray of sizzling canapés.

"And that's all you get, Mr. Queen, until the test is over,"
the oil man explained. "We don't eat dinner until afterward."

"The Arabs have a proverb," said Dr. Vreeland. "When
the stomach speaks, wisdom is silent."

"Or as Stevenson put it," murmured Miss Wandermere,
"the sort who eat unduly must never hope for glory."

"You see, Queen, we want you to be at your best," said
Darnell, the lawyer, staring piercingly at their victim. "Our
membership rules are quite harsh. For example, application
is by unanimous invitation only. Our fifth member, Dr. Arkavy, the Nobel Prize-winning biochemist, who's away at a
science conference, voted by cable all the way from Moscow
to invite you."

"You should understand, too," said Tycoon Syres, "that if
you fail to solve the puzzle we're going to throw at you tonight, you'll never be invited to try again."

"Harsh, indeed," said Ellery, nodding. "You titillate me. How exactly is the puzzle propounded?"

"In story form," said the lady poet. "How else?"

"Have I the option of asking questions?"

"As many as you like," said the little psychiatrist.

"In that case," Ellery said, "you-all may fire when ready."

"It happened during World War II," the multimillionaire host began the story. "You'll remember how hectic everything was—government departments mushrooming overnight, new bureaus scrambling to get organized, all sorts of people pulled out of the woodwork to help with the war effort, and security officers going crazy with the work load suddenly dumped on their shoulders."

"In a certain very important government war bureau newly set up," Psychiatrist Vreeland said as he lit a cigar, "one of the working force taken on was a little man named Tarleton, J. Aubrey Tarleton, who came out of retirement to do his bit for Uncle Sam. J. Aubrey was an ex-civil servant with a good if undistinguished record in government service. The bureau was an essential and very sensitive one. There was no time to do more than a conventional security check, but Tarleton's long record seemed to speak for itself."

"If you had seen old Mr. Tarleton," Miss Wandermere, the poet, took up the tale, "he would have struck you as a throwback—say, someone out of the British civil service in Rudyard Kipling's day. He had a Colonel Blimp mustache, he invariably dressed in ultraconservative clothes of Edwardian cut, he actually wore a piped vest and spats, carried a silverheaded cane, and he was never without a boutonnière pinned to his lapel, usually a white gardenia. A spic-and-span, courtly little old gentleman out of a long-dead age.

"His tastes were as elegantly old-fashioned," the lady poet went on, "as his manners. For instance, Mr. Tarleton was something of a gourmet and a connoisseur of vintages. Also, he would talk endlessly about his hobby, which was painting tiny landscapes on little ovals of ivory and ceramic—even worse, going on and on about his collection of Eighteenth Century miniatures by Richard Cosway and Ozias Humphry and other artists practically no one had ever heard of. In short, he was a good deal of a bore, and the younger people in the bureau especially vied with one another inventing new ways of avoiding him."

"Then something happened," Lawyer Darnell chimed in, "that threw the spotlight on little Mr. Tarleton. It was shortly before D-Day, and the dapper old gent suddenly wangled a priority airline passage to London. And just then Intelligence received an anonymous tip that Tarleton was in the pay of the Nazis—that he was a German spy. There were thousands of such tips during the war, most of them checking out as baseless, the result of malice, or spy fever, or what-have-you. But in view of Tarleton's access to top-secret material, and rather than take a chance at such a critical time, they yanked old Tarleton off the plane just as it was about to take off, and they gave him a going-over."

"This," asserted Oil Man Syres gravely, "was the most thorough search in the long and honorable history of spy-catching. It took a very long time, because at first it was entirely unsuccessful. In the end, of course, they found it."

"The plans for the Allied invasion of Europe, no doubt," Ellery said, smiling.

"Exactly," said Miss Wandermere, looking faintly disapproving. "The date cycle for D-Day, the location of the landings, the strength of the Allied forces—everything the German high command needed to smash the invasion in its tracks. There it was, to the last detail, all written down in plain uncoded English.

"The question you've got to answer, Mr. Queen, is a simple one. But watch out! Where did the Intelligence people find the spy message?"

"Or to put it the other way," Darnell, the criminal lawyer, said, "where did Tarleton conceal the spy message?"

"May I rule out the plane?" Ellery asked promptly. "That is, he didn't conceal it somewhere on board just before he was grabbed? Or in his luggage, or someone else's luggage?"

"He did not."

"He didn't pass it to a confederate?"

"No."

"The message was found on his person?"

"It was."

"Well, let's see." Ellery frowned. "I assume the obvious places of possible concealment yielded nothing—hat, coats, vest, trousers, shirt, tie, shoes, socks, spats, underclothing, galoshes or rubbers, that sort of thing?" There was a general nod. "The flower in his buttonhole? It was a real flower?"

"Nature's own," said Dr. Vreeland.

"The contents of his pockets?"

"Every object he carried in his pockets was minutely gone over, without result."

"The pockets themselves?"

"Concealed nothing."

"A secret pocket? Anywhere in his clothing?"

"No."

"Was he carrying a book?"

"No."

"A newspaper? Magazine? Directory? Any printed material whatever?"

"None."

"There must have been some printed matter in his wallet —credit cards, driver's license—"

"All carefully examined," Syres chuckled, "including, I might add, the material of the wallet itself—for secret writing. And no dice."

"Was his bare skin examined for secret writing?"

"It was, including his scalp, ears, and finger- and toenails," the oil man grinned, "and there wasn't any. They looked under infrared and ultraviolet and every other kind of light known to science. They peered at every square inch through a microscope. They used every chemical known to bring out secret writing. They even parboiled him—applied heat."

"Thorough," said Ellery dryly. "Well." He reflected. "Was he tattooed with some design that looked innocuous but actually concealed a hidden message?"

"In the naked state," Miss Wandermere assured him, "old Mr. Tarleton was as pinkly unmarred as a healthy six-month fetus."

"And I take it the usual fluoroscope and X-ray examinations were made without turning the message up in the old spy's interior?"

"You take it correctly, Mr. Queen."

"His mustache!" Ellery said. "Under it."

"Ingenious mind, this fellow," Lawyer Darnell said admiringly. "You mean Tarleton wrote the message on his upper lip and then grew a mustache over it? Well, Intelligence thought of that. They shaved off his mustache and found nothing underneath but lip."

"Interesting." Ellery was pulling on his nose, a sure sign of deep cerebration. "Let's tackle objects that might conceal the message. If I hit one that's relevant, stop me . . . Watch, wrist or pocket type? Ring? Hearing aid? Hairpiece? Glass eye? Contact lenses? The shafts of eyeglasses? False teeth? False finger or toe? Any prosthetic device at all?"

"Heavens, you'll have the old traitor made up of bits and pieces, Mr. Queen," laughed the lady poet. "No to all your suggestions."

"Key ring? Card case? Cufflinks? Tie clasp? Belt? Suspenders? Pipe? Tobacco pouch? Cigarets? Cigaret case? Snuffbox? Pillbox?" Ellery went on and on, until he ran out of ideas. To each suggestion they shook their heads.

There was silence. The members of The Puzzle Club glanced at one another significantly.

"Buttons," Ellery said, of a sudden. "Hollowed-out buttons! No? . . . Ah, I've forgotten something!"

"What's that?" asked Darnell curiously.

"His silver-headed cane!"

But they all shook their heads, smiling. And there was silence again.

"Well, I've eliminated everything you've told me about the old boy, and lots more. Or have I?"

"To that question, Mr. Queen," said Syres, smiling even more broadly, "you'll have to provide your own answer. Fascinating problem, isn't it?"

"And damned smart Intelligence people," Ellery mourned. "Final question: What if there's more than one answer, and I hit one you haven't thought of?"

There was incredulous hilarity.

"In that case," the lady poet said, "we'd probably elect you president of the Club."

"Now, Mr. Queen," said Syres, "you may retire to my study to think, or take a walk down Park Avenue, or spend your time any way you please while chewing on the puzzle. Unfortunately, we can't let you have more than an hour. My chef Charlot's dinner won't be edible after nine o'clock. Which is your pleasure?"

"Inasmuch as all this ratiocination has made me hungry," Ellery said, grinning back, "I think I'll answer your puzzle right now."

"The clue," Ellery chuckled in the attentive silence, "stemmed from old Tarleton's hobby—his painting of miniatures. It naturally suggested that he had written the spy message in miniature—in lettering so small it could be read only through a strong magnifying glass. That much was obvious.

"The question, of course, was: On which object Tarleton carried on his person was the miniaturized spy message inscribed?

"I just questioned whether I had covered everything about the old spy that you people had mentioned in your description of him. Of course I had not. I eliminated every possible object on Tarleton's person *but one*. The message must therefore have been written in miniature on that one object.

"Old Tarleton was in the tradition of the very select few who have been able to inscribe the Gettysburg Address or the

Lord's Prayer on an object no bigger than an oversized period.

"He wrote the spy message on the head of the pin that secured the flower to his lapel."

"Miss Wandermere and gentlemen," said the tycoon heartily, "I give you the newest member of The Puzzle Club!"

The President Regrets

The Puzzle Club is a congeries of very important people drawn together by unimportant purpose but common passion —to wit, to mystify one another. Their pleasure, in short, is puzzles.

Application is by invitation only, and membership must be won, the applicant having to submit to the Ordeal by Puzzle. If he survives the test, it earns him automatic admission.

Shortly after Ellery became The Puzzle Club's sixth regular member, it was proposed and unanimously voted to invite the President of the United States to apply for membership.

This was no frivolous motion; the members took their puzzles seriously, and the President was known to be a devotee of mysteries in all lawful forms. Besides, the Club's Founder and First Member, multimillionaire oil man Syres, had been buddy-buddy with the occupant of the White House since their youthful days as riggers in the Texas oilfields.

The invitation went to Washington, and rather to Ellery's surprise the President promptly accepted the challenge. In deference to affairs of state, he was urged to designate his own date, which he did; but when Ellery arrived at Syres's Park Avenue penthouse on the appointed evening to find the membership assembled, he was greeted with gloomy news. The President regretted that he could not make it after all. A Secret Service man, just departed, had brought the message that a new crisis in the Middle East had caused a last-minute cancellation of the President's flight to New York.

"What shall we do now?" asked Darnell, the famous criminal lawyer.

"There's no point in wasting the puzzle we've prepared for the President," said Dr. Vreeland, the well-known psychiatrist. "Let's save it for whenever he can get here."

"It's too bad Dr. Arkavy is still attending that symposium in Moscow," said wispy little Emmy Wandermere, the poet. Dr. Arkavy was the Nobel Prize-winning biochemist. "He has such a fertile mind, he can always come up with something on the spur of the moment."

"Maybe our newest member can help us out," said their Texan host. "What do you say, Queen? You must have a hundred problems at your fingers' ends, from your long experience as a writer and a detective."

"Let me think." Ellery cogitated. Then he chuckled. "All right. Give me a few minutes to work out the details . . ." It took him far less. "I'm ready. I suggest we engage in some collective improvisation, to begin with. Since this is going to be a murder mystery, we will obviously require a victim. Any suggestions?"

"A woman, of course," the lady poet said at once.

"Reeking of glamour," said the psychiatrist.

"That," said the criminal lawyer, "would seem to call for a Hollywood movie star."

"Good enough," Ellery said. "And a glamour girl of the screen calls for a glamourous name. Let's call her . . . oh, Valetta Van Buren. Agreed?"

"Valetta Van Buren." Miss Wandermere considered. "Yes. She personifies sex in her roles—a smoky witch with enormous cold, full-moon eyes. Does that follow, Mr. Queen?"

"Perfectly. Well, Valetta is in New York to attend the première of her latest picture and to do the circuit of TV appearances in promotion of it," Ellery went on. "But this hasn't proved an ordinary publicity tour. In fact, Valetta has had a frightening experience. It so shook her up that she wrote me an agitated letter about it which, by the magic of coincidence, I received just this morning."

"In which," Dr. Vreeland pressed, "she said—"

"That during this New York visit she permitted herself to be squired about town by four men—"

"Who are all, naturally, in love with her?" asked the lady poet.

"You guessed it, Miss Wandermere. She identified the four in her letter. One is that notorious man-about-town and play-boy, John Thrushbottom Taylor the Third—and if you haven't heard of Mr. Taylor, it's because I just made him up. The second is that wolf—in both senses—of Wall Street, named . . . well, let's call him A. Palmer Harrison. The third, of course, is the latest rage among society Pop Art painters, Leonardo Price. And the last of the quartet is—let's see—Biff Wilson, the professional football player."

"A likely story," grinned Oil Man Syres.

"Now." Ellery made a professional bridge of his fingers. "Having named the four men for me, Valetta went on to say that yesterday all four proposed marriage to her—each of them, on the same day. Unhappily, our ineffable Valetta felt nothing for any of them—nothing permanent, at any rate. She rejected all four impartially. It was a busy day for Miss Van Buren, and she would have enjoyed it except for one thing."

"One of them," said the criminal lawyer, "turned ugly."

"Exactly, Darnell. Valetta wrote me that three of them took their turndowns with approximate grace. But the fourth flew into a homicidal rage and threatened to kill her. She was terrified that he would try to carry out his threat and asked me to get in touch with her at once. She felt reluctant to go to the police, she wrote, because of the bad publicity it would bring her."

"What happened then?" asked Syres.

"I phoned, of course," Ellery replied, "as soon as I finished reading her letter. Would you believe it? I was too late. She was murdered last night, a short time after she must have mailed the letter. So the screen has lost its sexiest pot, and millions of red-blooded Americans at this very moment are mourning the sheer waste of it all."

"How," asked Darnell, "was the foul deed done?"

"I could tell you," Ellery said, "that she was done in by a Tasmanian yoyo, but I won't be unfair—the nature of the weapon is irrelevant. However, I will say this, to avoid complications: Valetta *was* murdered by the suitor who threatened her life."

"And is that all?" asked the tycoon.

"No, I've saved the kicker for last, Mr. Syres. Valetta's letter gave me one clue. In writing about the four men, she said that she'd noticed *she had something in common with three of the four,* and that the fourth was the one who had threatened her."

"Oh," said Dr. Vreeland. "Then all we have to establish is the nature of the common denominator. The three sharing it with Valetta would be innocent. By elimination, therefore, the one left over has to be the guilty man."

Ellery nodded. "And now—if my initiation at the last meeting was a criterion—the floor is open. Any questions?"

"I take it," the lady poet murmured, "that we may disregard the obvious possibilities of connection—that Valetta and three of the men were of the same age, or had the same color hair, or the same religious affiliation, or came from the same town or state, or attended the same college, or were investors or board members in the same corporation—that sort of thing?"

Ellery laughed. "Yes, you may disregard those."

"Social position?" the multimillionaire ventured. "Three of the men you described—Playboy John Something Taylor, Wall Street man A. Palmer Harrison, Pop Art Painter Price —did they all come from high society? That probably wouldn't be true of the pro football player, What's-His-Name."

"It just happened," Ellery mourned, 'that Pop Art Painter Price was born in a Greenwich Village pad. And Valetta, of course, hailed from the slums of Chicago."

They pondered.

"Had three of the four men ever served with Valetta," asked Darnell suddenly, "on the same jury?"

"No."

"On a TV panel show?" asked the poet quickly.

"No, Miss Wandermere."

"Don't tell me," said Dr. Vreeland, smiling, "that Valetta Van Buren and three of her suitors at one juncture in their lives shared the same psychiatrist's couch?"

"That's a good solution, Doctor. But it's not the solution I have in mind."

"Politics," the oil man said. "Valetta and three of the suitors are registered in the same party."

"My information, Mr. Syres," said Ellery, "is that Valetta was an incorrigible Democrat, the playboy and the Wall Street man are conservative Republicans, and Price and Biff Wilson never voted in their lives."

Miss Wandermere suddenly said, "It isn't anything like that. Am I right, Mr. Queen, in assuming that all the relevant facts were given to us in the body of your story?"

"I wondered when someone was going to ask that." Ellery chuckled. "That's exactly so, Miss Wandermere. There's really no need to ask questions at all."

"Then I for one need more time," said the tycoon. "What about the rest of you?" At their abstracted nods their host rose. "I suggest we make an exception tonight and eat Charlot's exquisite dinner before we crack Queen's puzzle."

Miss Wandermere's shocking blue eyes sparkled with enlightenmnet during Charlot's *moussaline de saumon*. Darnell's mustache-sized brows lifted with elation over the *suprêmes de volaille aux huîtres*. Dr. Vreeland uttered his self-congratulatory exclamation at the serving of the *selle de veau à l'Orientale*. And their host, Syres, achieved sweet victory over his *charlotte Chantilly*. But no one uttered a word until they were seated about the drawing room again over espresso and brandy.

"I detect from this and that," Ellery said, "that none of you encountered any real difficulty with my little puzzle."

"It's too bad the President had to miss this," Syres roared. "It was made to order, Queen, for his type of mind! Are you all quite ready?"

There was a universal nod.

"In that case," Ellery said, with resignation, "which of Valetta's four swains murdered her?"

"Females first, always," said Dr. Vreeland with a gallant nod to Miss Wandermere.

"The key to the answer," said the lady poet promptly, "consists in the fact, Mr. Queen, that you really told us just one thing about Valetta *and* her four suitors. It follows that whatever she and three of the four men had in common must relate to that thing."

"A logic I can't dispute," murmured Ellery. "And that thing was?"

Darnell grinned. "What the anticipation of the President's visit here tonight suggested to you when we asked for an impromptu puzzle. Their names."

"You named the movie star Valetta Van Buren," said Syres. *"Van Buren—the name of a President of the United States."*

"Then Playboy John Thrushbottom Taylor the Third," said the psychiatrist. "You buried that one, Queen! But of course Taylor is the name of a President of the United States, too—Zachary Taylor."

"And the Wall Street man, A. Palmer Harrison," the lawyer said. "Harrison—William Henry. Also Benjamin."

"And professional football player Biff Wilson." Miss Wandermere twinkled. "That 'Biff' was masterly, Mr. Queen. But —of course, Wilson, for Woodrow Wilson."

"And that leaves one character whose name," said the oil man, "bears no cross-reference to a President's name—Leonardo Price. So Price, the Pop Art painter, murdered Valetta. You almost had me fooled, Queen. Taylor, Van Buren, Harrison! That was tricky, picking the more obscure Presidents."

"You could hardly expect me to name one of my characters Eisenhower," Ellery grinned. "Which reminds me." He raised his brandy snifter. "Here's to our absent President—and may he turn out to be the next member of The Puzzle Club!"

HISTORICAL DETECTIVE STORY

Abraham Lincoln's Clue

Fourscore and eighteen years ago, Abraham Lincoln brought forth (in this account) a new notion, conceived in secrecy and dedicated to the proposition that even an Honest Abe may borrow a leaf from Edgar A. Poe.

It is altogether fitting and proper that Mr. Lincoln's venture into the detective story should come to its final resting place in the files of a man named Queen. For all his life Ellery has consecrated Father Abraham as the noblest projection of the American dream; and, insofar as it has been within his poor power to add or detract, he has given full measure of devotion, testing whether that notion, or any notion so conceived and so dedicated, deserves to endure.

Ellery's service in running the Lincoln clue to earth is one the world has little noted nor, perhaps, will long remember. That he shall not have served in vain, this account:

The case began on the outskirts of an upstate-New York city with the dreadful name of Eulalia, behind the flaking shutters of a fat and curlicued house with architectural dandruff, recalling for all the world some blowsy ex-Bloomer Girl from the Gay Nineties of its origin.

The owner, a formerly wealthy man named DiCampo, possessed a grandeur not shared by his property, although it was no less fallen into ruin. His falcon's face, more Florentine than Victorian, was—like the house—ravaged by time and the inclemencies of fortune; but haughtily so, and indeed DiCampo wore his scurfy purple velvet house jacket like the prince he was entitled to call himself, but did not. He was proud, and stubborn, and useless; and he had a lovely daughter named Bianca, who taught at a Eulalia grade school, and through marvels of economy, supported them both.

How Lorenzo San Marco Borghese-Ruffo DiCampo came to this decayed estate is no concern of ours. The presence there this day of a man named Harbidger and a man named Tungston, however, is to the point: they had come, Harbidger from Chicago, Tungston from Philadelphia, to buy something each wanted very much, and DiCampo had summoned them in order to sell it. The two visitors were collectors, Harbidger's passion being Lincoln, Tungston's Poe.

The Lincoln collector, an elderly man who looked like a migrant fruit picker, had plucked his fruits well: Harbidger was worth about $40,000,000, every dollar of which was at the beck of his mania for Lincolniana. Tungston, who was almost as rich, had the aging body of a poet and the eyes of a starving panther, armament that had served him well in the wars of Poeana.

"I must say, Mr. DiCampo," remarked Harbidger, "that your letter surprised me." He paused to savor the wine his host had poured from an ancient and honorable bottle (DiCampo had filled it with California claret before their arrival). "May I ask what has finally induced you to offer the book and document for sale?"

"To quote Lincoln in another context, Mr. Harbidger," said DiCampo with a shrug of his wasted shoulders, " 'the dogmas of the quiet past are inadequate to the stormy present.' In short, a hungry man sells his blood."

"Only if it's of the right type," said old Tungston, unmoved. "You've made that book and document less accessible to collectors and historians, DiCampo, than the gold in Fort Knox. Have you got them here? I'd like to examine them."

"No other hand will ever touch them except by right of ownership," Lorenzo DiCampo replied bitterly. He had taken a miser's glee in his lucky finds, vowing never to part with them; now forced by his need to sell them, he was like a suspicion-caked old prospector who, stumbling at last on pay dirt, draws cryptic maps to keep the world from stealing the secret of its location. "As I informed you gentlemen, I represent the book as bearing the signatures of Poe and Lincoln, and the document as being in Lincoln's hand; I am offering them with the customary proviso that they are returnable if they should prove to be not as represented; and if this does not satisfy you," and the old prince actually rose, "let us terminate our business here and now."

"Sit down, sit down, Mr. DiCampo," Harbidger said.

"No one is questioning your integrity," snapped old Tungston. "It's just that I'm not used to buying sight unseen. If there's a money-back guarantee, we'll do it your way."

Lorenzo DiCampo reseated himself stiffly. "Very well, gentlemen. Then I take it you are both prepared to buy?"

"Oh, yes!" said Harbidger. "What is your price?"

"Oh, no," said DiCampo. "What is your bid?"

The Lincoln collector cleared his throat, which was full of slaver. "If the book and document are as represented, Mr. DiCampo, you might hope to get from a dealer or realize at auction—oh—$50,000. I offer you $55,000."

"$56,000," said Tungston.

"$57,000," said Harbidger.

"$58,000," said Tungston.

"$59,000," said Harbidger."

Tungston showed his fangs. "$60,000," he said.

Harbidger fell silent, and DiCampo waited. He did not expect miracles. To these men, five times $60,000 was of less moment than the undistinguished wine they were smacking their lips over; but they were veterans of many a hard auction-room campaign, and a collector's victory tastes very nearly as sweet for the price as for the prize.

So the impoverished prince was not surprised when the Lincoln collector suddenly said, "Would you be good enough to allow Mr. Tungston and me to talk privately for a moment?"

DiCampo rose and strolled out of the room, to gaze somberly through a cracked window at the jungle growth that had once been his Italian formal gardens.

It was the Poe collector who summoned him back. "Harbidger has convinced me that for the two of us to try to outbid each other would simply run the price up out of all reason. We're going to make you a sporting proposition."

"I've proposed to Mr. Tungston, and he has agreed," nodded Harbidger, "that our bid for the book and document be $65,000. Each of us is prepared to pay that sum, and not a penny more."

"So that is how the screws are turned," said DiCampo, smiling. "But I do not understand. If each of you makes the identical bid, which of you gets the book and document?"

"Ah," grinned the Poe man, "that's where the sporting proposition comes in."

"You see, Mr. DiCampo," said the Lincoln man, "we are going to leave that decision to you."

Even the old prince, who had seen more than his share of

the astonishing, was astonished. He looked at the two rich
men really for the first time. "I must confess," he murmured,
"that your compact is an amusement. Permit me?" He sank
into thought while the two collectors sat expectantly. When
the old man looked up he was smiling like a fox. "The very
thing, gentlemen! From the typewritten copies of the document I sent you, you both know that Lincoln himself left a
clue to a theoretical hiding place for the book which he never
explained. Some time ago I arrived at a possible solution to
the President's little mystery. I propose to hide the book and
document in accordance with it."

"You mean whichever of us figures out your interpretation
of the Lincoln clue and finds the book and document where
you will hide them, Mr. DiCampo, gets both for the agreed
price?"

"That is it exactly."

The Lincoln collector looked dubious. "I don't know . . ."

"Oh, come, Harbidger," said Tungston, eyes glittering. "A
deal is a deal. We accept, DiCampo! Now what?"

"You gentlemen will of course have to give me a little
time. Shall we say three days?"

        Ellery let himself into the Queen apartment, tossed his
suitcase aside, and set about opening windows. He had been
out of town for a week on a case, and Inspector Queen was
in Atlantic City attending a police convention.

Breathable air having been restored, Ellery sat down to the
week's accumulation of mail. One envelope made him pause.
It had come by air-mail special delivery, it was postmarked
four days earlier, and in the lower left corner, in red, flamed
the word URGENT. The printed return address on the flap
said: *L.S.M.B.-R. DiCampo, Post Office Box 69, Southern
District, Eulalia, N.Y.* The initials of the name had been
crossed out and "Bianca" written above them.

The enclosure, in a large agitated female hand on inexpen-
sive notepaper, said:

Dear Mr. Queen,
    The most important detective book in the world has
disappeared. Will you please find it for me?
    Phone me on arrival at the Eulalia RR station or air-
port and I will pick you up.

                                Bianca DiCampo

A yellow envelope then caught his eye. It was a telegram,
dated the previous day:

WHY HAVE I NOT HEARD FROM YOU STOP AM IN DESPER-
ATE NEED YOUR SERVICES

                                        BIANCA DICAMPO

He had no sooner finished reading the telegram than the
telephone on his desk trilled. It was a long-distance call.

"Mr. Queen?" throbbed a contralto voice. "Thank heaven
I've finally got through to you! I've been calling all day—"

"I've been away," said Ellery, "and you would be Miss
Bianca DiCampo of Eulalia. In two words, Miss DiCampo:
Why me?"

"In two words, Mr. Queen: Abraham Lincoln."

Ellery was startled. "You plead a persuasive case," he
chuckled. "It's true, I'm an incurable Lincoln addict. How
did you find out? Well, never mind. Your letter refers to a
book, Miss DiCampo. Which book?"

The husky voice told him, and certain other provocative
things as well. "So will you come, Mr. Queen?"

"Tonight if I could! Suppose I drive up first thing in the
morning. I ought to make Eulalia by noon. Harbidger and
Tungston are still around, I take it?"

"Oh, yes. They're staying at a motel downtown."

"Would you ask them to be there?"

The moment he hung up Ellery leaped to his bookshelves.
He snatched out his volume of *Murder for Pleasure,* the his-
torical work on detective stories by his good friend Howard
Haycraft, and found what he was looking for on page 26:

And . . . young William Dean Howells thought it significant praise to assert of a nominee for President of
the United States:

The bent of his mind is mathematical and meta-
physical, and he is therefore pleased with the absolute and logical method of Poe's tales and sketches,
in which the problem of mystery is given, and
wrought out into everyday facts by processes of
cunning analysis. It is said that he suffers no year to
pass without a perusal of this author.

Abraham Lincoln subsequently confirmed this statement,
which appeared in his little-known "campaign biogra-
phy" by Howells in 1860 . . . The instance is chiefly
notable, of course, for its revelation of a little-suspected
affinity between two great Americans . . .

*   *   *

Very early the next morning Ellery gathered some papers from his files, stuffed them into his briefcase, scribbled a note for his father, and ran for his car, Eulalia-bound.

He was enchanted by the DiCampo house, which looked like something out of Poe by Charles Addams; and, for other reasons, by Bianca, who turned out to be a genetic product supreme of northern Italy, with titian hair and Mediterranean blue eyes and a figure that needed only some solid steaks to qualify her for Miss Universe competition. Also, she was in deep mourning; so her conquest of the Queen heart was immediate and complete.

"He died of a cerebral hemorrhage, Mr. Queen," Bianca said, dabbing her absurd little nose. "In the middle of the second night after his session with Mr. Harbidger and Mr. Tungston."

So Lorenzo San Marco Borghese-Ruffo DiCampo was unexpectedly dead, bequeathing the lovely Bianca near-destitution and a mystery.

"The only things of value father really left me are that book and the Lincoln document. The $65,000 they now represent would pay off father's debts and give me a fresh start. But I can't find them, Mr. Queen, and neither can Mr. Harbidger and Mr. Tungston—who'll be here soon, by the way. Father hid the two things, as he told them he would; but where? We've ransacked the place."

"Tell me more about the book, Miss DiCampo."

"As I said over the phone, it's called *The Gift: 1845*. The Christmas annual that contained the earliest appearance of Edgar Allan Poe's *The Purloined Letter*."

"Published in Philadelphia by Carey & Hart? Bound in red?" At Bianca's nod Ellery said, "You understand that an ordinary copy of *The Gift: 1845* isn't worth more than about $50. What makes your father's copy unique is that double autograph you mentioned."

"That's what he said, Mr. Queen. I wish I had the book here to show you—that beautifully handwritten *Edgar Allan Poe* on the flyleaf, and under Poe's signature the signature *Abraham Lincoln*."

"Poe's own copy, once owned, signed, and read by Lincoln," Ellery said slowly. "Yes, that would be a collector's item for the ages. By the way, Miss DiCampo, what's the story behind the other piece—the Lincoln document?"

Bianca told him what her father had told her.

One morning in the spring of 1865, Abraham Lincoln opened the rosewood door of his bedroom in the southwest corner of the second floor of the White House and stepped out into the red-carpeted hall at the unusually late hour—for him—of 7:00 A.M.; he was more accustomed to beginning his work day at six.

But (as Lorenzo DiCampo had reconstructed events) Mr. Lincoln that morning had lingered in his bedchamber. He had awakened at his usual hour but, instead of leaving immediately on dressing for his office, he had pulled one of the cane chairs over to the round table, with its gas-fed reading lamp, and sat down to reread Poe's *The Purloined Letter* in his copy of the 1845 annual; it was a dreary morning, and the natural light was poor. The President was alone; the folding doors to Mrs. Lincoln's bedroom remained closed.

Impressed as always with Poe's tale, Mr. Lincoln on this occasion was struck by a whimsical thought; and, apparently finding no paper handy, he took an envelope from his pocket, discarded its enclosure, slit the two short edges so that the envelope opened out into a single sheet, and began to write on the blank side.

"Describe it to me, please."

"It's a long envelope, one that must have contained a bulky letter. It is addressed to the White House, but there is no return address, and father was never able to identify the sender from the handwriting. We do know that the letter came through the regular mails, because there are two Lincoln stamps on it, lightly but unmistakably canceled."

"May I see your father's transcript of what Lincoln wrote out that morning on the inside of the envelope?"

Bianca handed him a typewritten copy and, in spite of himself, Ellery felt goose flesh rise as he read:

Apr. 14, 1865

Mr. Poe's The Purloined Letter is a work of singular originality. Its simplicity is a master-stroke of cunning, which never fails to arouse my wonder.

Reading the tale over this morning has given me a "notion." Suppose I wished to hide a book, this very book, perhaps? Where best to do so? Well, as Mr. Poe in his tale hid a letter *among letters,* might not a book be hidden *among books?* Why, if this very copy of the tale were to be deposited in a library and on purpose not recorded—would not the Library of Congress make a prime depository!—well might it repose there, undiscovered, for a generation.

On the other hand, let us regard Mr. Poe's "notion" turn-about: Suppose the book were to be placed, not

amongst other books, but *where no book would reasonably be expected?* (I may follow the example of Mr. Poe,
and, myself, compose a tale of "ratiocination"!)

The "notion" beguiles me, it is nearly seven o'clock.
Later to-day, if the vultures and my appointments leave
me a few moments of leisure, I may write further of my
imagined hiding-place.

In self-reminder: The hiding-place of the book is in
30d, which

Ellery looked up. "The document ends there?"

"Father said that Mr. Lincoln must have glanced again at
his watch, and shamefacedly jumped up to go to his office,
leaving the sentence unfinished. Evidently he never found the
time to get back to it."

Ellery brooded. Evidently indeed. From the moment when
Abraham Lincoln stepped out of his bedroom that Good Friday morning, fingering his thick gold watch on its vest chain,
to bid the still-unrelieved night guard his customary cour-
teous "Good morning" and make for his office at the other
end of the hall, his day was spoken for. The usual patient
push through the clutching crowd of favor-seekers, many of
whom had bedded down all night on the hall carpet; sanc-
tuary in his sprawling office, where he read official correspondence; by 8:00 A.M. having breakfast with his family—Mrs.
Lincoln chattering away about plans for the evening, 12-
year-old Tad of the cleft palate lisping a complaint that "nobody asked me to go," and young Robert Lincoln, just returned from duty, bubbling with stories about his hero Ulys-
ses Grant and the last days of the war; then back to the presi-
dential office to look over the morning newspapers (which
Lincoln had once remarked he "never" read, but these were
happy days, with good news everywhere), sign two documents, and signal the soldier at the door to admit the morning's first caller, Speaker of the House Schuyler Colfax (who
was angling for a Cabinet post and had to be tactfully handled); and so on throughout the day—the historic Cabinet
meeting at 11:00 A.M., attended by General Grant himself,
that stretched well into the afternoon; a hurried lunch at almost half-past two with Mrs. Lincoln (had this 45-pounds-
underweight man eaten his usual midday meal of a biscuit, a
glass of milk, and an apple?); more visitors to see in his office (including the unscheduled Mrs. Nancy Bushrod, escaped
slave and wife of an escaped slave and mother of three small
children, weeping that Tom, a soldier in the Army of the Po-
tomac, was no longer getting his pay: "You are entitled to

your husband's pay. Come this time tomorrow," and the tall President escorted her to the door, bowing her out "like I was a natural-born lady"); the late afternoon drive in the barouche to the Navy Yard and back with Mrs. Lincoln; more work, more visitors, into the evening . . . until finally, at five minutes past 8:00 P.M., Abraham Lincoln stepped into the White House formal coach after his wife, waved, and sank back to be driven off to see a play he did not much want to see, *Our American Cousin,* at Ford's Theatre . . .

Ellery mused over that black day in silence. And, like a relative hanging on the specialist's yet undelivered diagnosis, Bianca DiCampo sat watching him with anxiety.

Harbidger and Tungston arrived in a taxi to greet Ellery with the fervor of castaways grasping at a smudge of smoke on the horizon.

"As I understand it, gentlemen," Ellery said when he had calmed them down, "neither of you has been able to solve Mr. DiCampo's interpretation of the Lincoln clue. If I succeed in finding the book and paper where DiCampo hid them, which of you gets them?"

"We intend to split the $65,000 payment to Miss Di-Campo," said Harbidger, "and take joint ownership of the two pieces."

"An arrangement," growled old Tungston, "I'm against on principle, in practice, and by plain horse sense."

"So am I," sighed the Lincoln collector, "but what else can we do?"

"Well," and the Poe man regarded Bianca DiCampo with the icy intimacy of the cat that long ago marked the bird as its prey, "Miss DiCampo, who now owns the two pieces, is quite free to renegotiate a sale on her own terms."

"Miss DiCampo," said Miss DiCampo, giving Tungston stare for stare, "considers herself bound by her father's wishes. His terms stand."

"In all likelihood, then," said the other millionaire, "one of us will retain the book, the other the document, and we'll exchange them every year, or some such thing." Harbidger sounded unhappy.

"Only practical arrangement under the circumstances," grunted Tungston, and *he* sounded unhappy. "But all this is academic, Queen, unless and until the book and document are found."

Ellery nodded. "The problem, then, is to fathom Di-Campo's interpretation of that *30d* in the document. 30d . . . I notice, Miss DiCampo—or, may I? Bianca?—that your fa-

ther's typewritten copy of the Lincoln holograph text runs the
3 and 0 and *d* together—no spacing in between. Is that the way
it occurs in the longhand?"

"Yes."

"Hmm. Still . . . 30d . . . Could *d* stand for *days* . . . or
the British *pence* . . . or *died*, as used in obituaries? Does
any of these make sense to you, Bianca?"

"No."

"Did your father have any special interest in, say, pharma-
cology? chemistry? physics? algebra? electricity? Small *d* is an
abbreviation used in all those." But Bianca shook her splen-
did head. "Banking? Small *d* for *dollars, dividends?*"

"Hardly," the girl said with a sad smile.

"How about theatricals? Was your father ever involved in
a play production? Small *d* stands for *door* in playscript stage
directions."

"Mr. Queen, I've gone through every darned abbreviation
my dictionary lists, and I haven't found one that has a point
of contact with any interest of my father's."

Ellery scowled. "At that—I assume the typewritten copy is
accurate—the manuscript shows no period after the *d*, making an abbreviation unlikely. 30d . . . let's concentrate on the
number. Does the number 30 have any significance for you?"

"Yes, indeed," said Bianca, making all three men sit up.
But then they sank back. "In a few years it will represent
my age, and that has enormous significance. But only for me,
I'm afraid."

"You'll be drawing wolf whistles at twice thirty," quoth Ellery warmly. "However! Could the number have cross-re-
ferred to anything in your father's life or habits?"

"None that I can think of, Mr. Queen. And," Bianca said,
having grown roses in her cheeks, "thank you."

"I think," said old Tungston testily, "we had better stick to
the subject."

"Just the same, Bianca, let me run over some 'thirty' asso-
ciations as they come to mind. Stop me if one of them hits a
nerve. The Thirty Tyrants—was your father interested in
classical Athens? Thirty Years' War—in Seventeenth Century
European history? Thirty all—did he play or follow tennis?
Or . . . did he ever live at an address that included the number 30?"

Ellery went on and on, but to each suggestion Bianca Di-
Campo could only shake her head.

"The lack of spacing, come to think of it, doesn't necessarily mean that Mr. DiCampo chose to view the clue that

way," said Ellery thoughtfully. "He might have interpreted it arbitrarily as *3-space-o-d.*"

"Three od?" echoed old Tungston. "What the devil could that mean?"

"Od? Od is the hypothetical force or power claimed by Baron von Reichenbach—in 1850, wasn't it?—to pervade the whole of nature. Manifests itself in magnets, crystals, and such, which according to the excited Baron explained animal magnetism and mesmerism. Was your father by any chance interested in hypnosis, Bianca? Or the occult?"

"Not in the slightest."

"Mr. Queen," exclaimed Harbidger, "are you serious about all this—this semantic sludge?"

"Why, I don't know," said Ellery. "I never know till I stumble over something. Od . . . the word was used with prefixes, too—*biod,* the force of animal life; *elod,* the force of electricity; and so forth. *Three* od . . . or *triod,* the triune force—it's all right, Mr. Harbidger, it's not ignorance on your part, I just coined the word. But it does rather suggest the Trinity, doesn't it? Bianca, did your father tie up to the Church in a personal, scholarly, or any other way? No? That's too bad, really, because Od—capitalized—has been a minced form of the word God since the Sixteenth Century. Or . . . you wouldn't happen to have three Bibles on the premises, would you? Because—"

Ellery stopped with the smashing abruptness of an ordinary force meeting an absolutely immovable object. The girl and the two collectors gawped. Bianca had idly picked up the typewritten copy of the Lincoln document. She was not reading it, she was simply holding it on her knees; but Ellery, sitting opposite her, had shot forward in a crouch, rather like a pointer, and he was regarding the paper in her lap with a glare of pure discovery.

"That's it!" he cried.

"What's it, Mr. Queen?" the girl asked, bewildered.

"Please—the transcript!" He plucked the paper from her. "Of course. Hear this: 'On the other hand, let us regard Mr. Poe's "notion" turn-about.' *Turn-about.* Look at the 30d 'turn-about'—as I just saw it!"

He turned the Lincoln message upside down for their inspection. In that position the 30d became:

P0ε

"*Poe!*" exploded Tungston.

"Yes, crude but recognizable," Ellery said swiftly. "So now

we read the Lincoln clue as: 'The hiding-place of the book is in *Poe*'!"

There was a silence.

"In Poe," said Harbidger blankly.

"In Poe?" muttered Tungston. "There are only a couple of trade editions of Poe in DiCampo's library, Harbidger, and we went through those. We looked in every book here."

"He might have meant among the Poe books in the *public* library. Miss DiCampo—"

"Wait." Bianca sped away. But when she came back she was drooping. "It isn't. We have two public libraries in Eulalia, and I know the head librarian in both. I just called them. Father didn't visit either library."

Ellery gnawed a fingernail. "Is there a bust of Poe in the house, Bianca? Or any other Poe-associated object, aside from books?"

"I'm afraid not."

"Queer," he mumbled. "Yet I'm positive your father interpreted 'the hiding-place of the book' as being 'in Poe.' So he'd have hidden it 'in Poe' . . ."

Ellery's mumbling dribbled away into a tormented sort of silence: his eyebrows worked up and down, Groucho Marx fashion; he pinched the tip of his nose until it was scarlet; he yanked at his unoffending ears; he munched on his lip . . . until, all at once, his face cleared; and he sprang to his feet. "Bianca, may I use your phone?"

The girl could only nod, and Ellery dashed. They heard him telephoning in the entrance hall, although they could not make out the words. He was back in two minutes.

"One thing more," he said briskly, "and we're out of the woods. I suppose your father had a key ring or a key case, Bianca? May I have it, please?"

She fetched a key case. To the two millionaires it seemed the sorriest of objects, a scuffed and dirty tan leatherette case. But Ellery received it from the girl as if it were an artifact of historic importance from a newly discovered IV Dynasty tomb. He unsnapped it with concentrated love; he fingered its contents like a scientist. Finally he decided on a certain key.

"Wait here!" Thus Mr. Queen; and exit, running.

"I can't decide," old Tungston said after a while, "whether that fellow is a genius or an escaped lunatic."

Neither Harbidger nor Bianca replied. Apparently they could not decide, either.

They waited through twenty elongated minutes; at the twenty-first they heard his car, champing. All three were in the front doorway as Ellery strode up the walk.

He was carrying a book with a red cover, and smiling. It was a compassionate smile, but none of them noticed.

"You—" said Bianca. "—found—" said Tungston. "—the book!" shouted Harbidger. "Is the Lincoln holograph in it?"

"It is," said Ellery. "Shall we all go into the house, where we may mourn in decent privacy?"

"Because," Ellery said to Bianca and the two quivering collectors as they sat across a refectory table from him, "I have foul news. Mr. Tungston, I believe you have never actually seen Mr. DiCampo's book. Will you now look at the Poe signature on the flyleaf?"

The panther claws leaped. There, toward the top of the flyleaf, in faded inkscript, was the signature *Edgar Allan Poe*. The claws curled, and old Tungston looked up sharply. "DiCampo never mentioned that it's a full autograph—he kept referring to it as 'the Poe signature.' Edgar *Allan* Poe . . . Why, I don't know of a single instance after his West Point days when Poe wrote out his middle name in an autograph! And the earliest he could have signed this 1845 edition is obviously when it was published, which was around the fall of 1844. In 1844 he'd surely have abbreviated the 'Allan,' signing 'Edgar *A*. Poe,' the way he signed everything! This is a forgery."

"My God," murmured Bianca, clearly intending no impiety; she was as pale as Poe's Lenore. "Is that true, Mr. Queen?"

"I'm afraid it is," Ellery said sadly. "I was suspicious the moment you told me the Poe signature on the flyleaf contained the 'Allan.' And if the Poe signature is a forgery, the book itself can hardly be considered Poe's own copy."

Harbidger was moaning. "And the Lincoln signature underneath the Poe, Mr. Queen! DiCampo never told me it reads *Abraham* Lincoln—the full Christian name. Except on official documents, Lincoln practically always signed his name '*A*. Lincoln.' Don't tell me this Lincoln autograph is a forgery, too?"

Ellery forbore to look at poor Bianca. "I was struck by the 'Abraham' as well, Mr. Harbidger, when Miss DiCampo mentioned it to me, and I came equipped to test it. I have here"—and Ellery tapped the pile of documents he had taken from his briefcase—"facsimiles of Lincoln signatures from the most frequently reproduced of the historic documents he signed. Now I'm going to make a precise tracing of the Lincoln signature on the flyleaf of the book"—he proceeded to do so—"and I shall superimpose the tracing on the various signatures of the authentic Lincoln documents. So."

He worked rapidly. On his third superimposition Ellery looked up. "Yes. See here. The tracing of the purported Lincoln signature from the flyleaf fits in minutest detail over the authentic Lincoln signature on this facsimile of the Emancipation Proclamation. It's a fact of life that's tripped many a forger that *nobody ever writes his name exactly the same way twice.* There are always variations. If two signatures are identical, then, one must be a tracing of the other. So the 'Abraham Lincoln' signed on this flyleaf can be dismissed without further consideration as a forgery also. It's a tracing of the Emancipation Proclamation signature.

"Not only was this book not Poe's own copy; it was never signed—and therefore probably never owned—by Lincoln. However your father came into possession of the book, Bianca, he was swindled."

It was the measure of Bianca DiCampo's quality that she said quietly. "Poor, poor father," nothing more.

Harbidger was poring over the worn old envelope on whose inside appeared the dearly beloved handscript of the Martyr President. "At least," he muttered, "we have *this.*"

"Do we?" asked Ellery gently. "Turn it over, Mr. Harbidger."

Harbidger looked up, scowling. "No! You're not going to deprive me of this, too!"

"Turn it over," Ellery repeated in the same gentle way. The Lincoln collector obeyed reluctantly. "What do you see?"

"An authentic envelope of the period! With two authentic Lincoln stamps!"

"Exactly And the United States has never issued postage stamps depicting living Americans; you have to be dead to qualify The earliest U.S. stamp showing a portrait of Lincoln went on sale April 15, 1866—a year to the day after his death. Then a living Lincoln could scarcely have used this envelope, with these stamps on it, as writing paper. The document is spurious, too. I am so very sorry, Bianca."

Incredibly, Lorenzo DiCampo's daughter managed a smile with her *"Non importa, signor."* He could have wept for her. As for the two collectors, Harbidger was in shock; but old Tungston managed to croak, "Where the devil did DiCampo hide the book, Queen? And how did you know?"

"Oh, that," said Ellery, wishing the two old men would go away so that he might comfort this admirable creature. "I was convinced that DiCampo interpreted what we now know was the forger's, not Lincoln's, clue, as *30d* read upside down; or, crudely, *Poe*. But 'the hiding-place of the book is in Poe' led nowhere.

"So I reconsidered, P, o, e. If those three letters of the alphabet didn't meant Poe, what could they mean? Then I remembered something about the letter you wrote me, Bianca. You'd used one of your father's envelopes, on the flap of which appeared his address: *Post Office Box 69, Southern District, Eulalia, N.Y.* If there was a Southern District in Eulalia, it seemed reasonable to conclude that there were post offices for other points of the compass, too. As, for instance, an Eastern District. Post Office Eastern, P.O. East. P.O.E."

"Poe!" cried Bianca.

"To answer your question, Mr. Tungston: I phoned the main post office, confirmed the existence of a Post Office East, got directions as to how to get there, looked for a postal box key in Mr. DiCampo's key case, found the right one, located the box DiCampo had rented especially for the occasion, unlocked it—and there was the book." He added, hopefully, "And that is that."

"And that *is* that," Bianca said when she returned from seeing the two collectors off. "I'm not going to cry over an empty milk bottle, Mr. Queen. I'll straighten out father's affairs somehow. Right now all I can think of is how glad I am he didn't live to see the signatures and documents declared forgeries publicly, as they would surely have been when they were expertized."

"I think you'll find there's still some milk in the bottle, Bianca."

"I beg your pardon?" said Bianca.

Ellery tapped the pseudo-Lincolnian envelope. "You know, you didn't do a very good job describing this envelope to me. All you said was that there were two canceled Lincoln stamps on it."

"Well, there are."

"I can see you misspent your childhood. No, little girls don't collect things, do they? Why, if you'll examine these 'two canceled Lincoln stamps,' you'll see that they're a great deal more than that. In the first place, they're not separate stamps. They're a vertical pair—that is, one stamp is joined to the other at the horizontal edges. Now look at this upper stamp of the pair."

The Mediterranean eyes widened. "It's upside down, isn't it?"

"Yes, it's upside down," said Ellery, "and what's more,

while the pair have perforations all around, there are no perforations between them, where they're joined.

"What you have here, young lady—and what our unknown forger didn't realize when he fished around for an authentic White House cover of the period on which to perpetrate the Lincoln forgery—is what stamp collectors might call a double printing error: a pair of 1866 black 15-cent Lincolns imperforate horizontally, with one of the pair printed upside down. No such error of the Lincoln issue has ever been reported. You're the owner, Bianca, of what may well be the rarest item in U.S. philately, and the most valuable."

The world will little note, nor long remember.

But don't try to prove it by Bianca DiCampo.